ORC'S MAIDEN

MONSTER MATE HUNT, BOOK 3

AVA ROSS

ENCHANTED STAR PRESS

For my own special hero,
my husband, Rusty.

MONSTER MATE HUNT TERMS, CHARACTERS, & GENERAL INFORMATION

Orc's Mate (takes place 5 years before Orc's Craving):

Zephyr Clan: Air. Pendant is a circular disc made up of swirls to represent the air and water

Characters: Odik Brunellon, Eleri. Their children: Zur, Yusta

Birgid: woman who taunts Eleri and murdered Zur, the hunter who raised Eleri

Cassatine: orc midwife

Crikin: Dakur's father

Drabass: male from Odik's clan

Madine: elderly orc female; the keeper of clan stories

Trilden: Odik's friend

Zarran: Odik's vox

Zur: elderly man who adopted Eleri. They name their son after him

Orc's Craving, Book 1

Azuris Clan: Water/Sea. Pendant: metal swirls with spikes resembling waves

Characters: Rhoslyn, Jaus Kreedaull, Shirra: their daughter

Arkest: oldest, most revered healer

Eamon: village mayor who wants Rhoslyn for himself

Feyla: Jaus' female vox

Kael: older guardsman

King Surled: Jaus & Madr's father

Liall: older orc who runs an herb shop in the orc city

Lyneth: Rhoslyn's sister; married to Sveth

Mastivule: head of the kingdom's guards

Viskeete: rather crude orc

Orc's Fate, Book 2

Lumen Clan: sun/mountains. Pendant: shaped like the sun, it represents the mountains and the heavens above

Characters: Madr Thourand, Lyneth

Brakkis: Madr's vox

Finsteg: Matis Clan male who challenges Madr

Grock: Azuris clan male who guards Lyneth and is murdered

Kael: older village guardsman, friend to Lyneth

Milllamay: shayde Dakur raised

Pulost: Matis Clan male who challenges Madr

Riank: Madr's cousin who wishes to rule

Sessavia: Matis Clan female, welcomes Lyneth

Taen: shayde Dakur raised

Tenkaril: Madr's mother, adopted Zickar; wise woman who "sees" when she touches someone

Tescall: Riank's younger brother and ally

Orc's Maiden, Book 3

Matis Clan: forest. Pendant: spikes from the sun like sunlight stabbing through the canopy

Characters: Zickar, Alwen, their son: Ferrin

Bredar: Alwen's brother

Brillie: Flazant female

Creea: Alwen's sister

Dillu: Flazant male

Loobek: orc male who went looking for Dakur

Mavileen: human woman, leader of the village on the edge of the forest

Nayleen: Alwen's sister

Noul: one of three shaydes Dakur raised

Pirrah: Flazant elder

Roolina: Alwen's mother

Rusket: older orc male

Trillie: Flazant female

Ulong: orc metal worker

Villadeer: Flazant female

Wambak: Flazant male

Orc's Captive, Book 4

Matis Clan

Characters: Dakur, Nia

Brunt: Nia's stepbrother

Kengart: head of Brunt's guards

Lianire: Brunt's second in command

Veegar: human male, cook

Woobedon: Nia's village built in the middle of the vast desert, near an oasis

Orc's Taming, Book 5

Ember Clan: desert/fire. Pendant: flames shooting toward the sky

Characters: Turren, Kaila

Airest: Turren's vox

Brunnen: Kaila's younger brother

Daskin: Turren's second in command

Ferella: female orc, Ember Clan

Gromget: orc game that's a mix of soccer and American football

Jabon: Kaila's boss in the village

Nuark: teenage orc living in the Ember Clan

Reven: teenage orc living in the Matis Clan

Sianna: orcling infant

Urlain: elder in the Ember Clan

Varalar: female smithy at the village

Vox history: Winged creatures fostered in the Ember Clan and bonded with orcs. They form within a seed and when they slip out, they bond with the person closest to them. In earlier days, this was their parent, but now all eligible males and females travel to the Ember clan to be there for the hatching. The bonded orc remains with the hatchling long enough for the vox to grow for flight, feeding and grooming it so it knows their touch and smell. They nest near their bonded orc but return to the Ember territory every three years when they're ready to produce young.

General Terms:

Ashenclaw: creature like a wolf

Aspest berries: found on Odik's island, can be added to tea

Avestilar: large birds who nest high in the canopy

Boolong: creature like a wild cow

Brugel: meat like bacon

Caedos: leader of a clan

Chall: like a cat; kits are their young

Cheerish: type of bird

Clik: distance; about a mile

Daphoon: a dolphin-like sea creature

Doonet: a light cloth made from a plant

Dresalod: vicious, enormous crab-like sea creatures that attack the orc city

Elkern: timid creature like a deer

Effervast trees: fragrant

Emerest stone: rare, found in caverns, Turren compares the color to Kaira's eyes when she's angry

Fillawate: drink made from a rare fruit that grows

deep beneath the ground. When fermented and drank, makes someone feel happy, though it's not alcohol

Flazant: stone people born of the boulders around us. Prior allies to the orcs

Hilardep: enormous, venomous spider found in the forest

Lamest: forest snake

Liladek flowers: lovely scent, bloom at night

Lindenmint: herb Rhoslyn drinks as tea; has antibacterial properties, slows a cut's blood flow. Found to be highly toxic to dresalods

Mellabar: a fruit jam

Orcling: orc baby/child

Reskit: creature like a rabbit

Ribber: creature like a rat

Secondist: Tuesday

Shayde: large, vicious, lizard-like creatures who live and hunt in the forest

Sinderfluff: material like silk

Squitt: creature like a squirrel

Succire, a sweet red berry

Tartledge Sea: vast, purple sea beyond the Orc Kingdom

Teegar: plants used to propel orcs to canopy platforms or take them below ground. Serve as elevators. Fed with diluted fillawate.

Teetser: a fly/mosquito

Trulist: trees that grow in thick groves

Wanderer: orc who travels, learning new ways to use their pendants

Weelen leaves: used in tea

Whisp: an insect that, when blown across, lights up. Used in lanterns as a source of light.

Willadon: a black root, made into a tea that relieves arthritis pain

Also by Ava Ross

Series by AVA

Mail-Order Brides of Crakair

Brides of Driegon

Fated Mates of the Ferlaern Warriors

Fated Mates of the Xilan Warriors

Holiday with a Cu'zod Warrior

Galaxy Games

Alien Warrior Abandoned

Beastly Alien Boss

Bride of the Fae

A Sci-Fi Holiday Tail

Monsterville, USA

Monster on Board

(co-written with Alana Khan)

Love at First Orc

Monster Mate Hunt

Sweet Monster Treats

Brides of the Zuldrux Warriors

Monsters, PI

Single Titles

A Monster Worth Fighting For

Craving Stardust

Dad Bod Dragon

Mated to the Dragon

Swamp Thing (You Make My Heart Sing)

Jasmine's Enchanted Genie

You can find her books on Amazon.

ORC'S MAIDEN

I'm determined to control my own life—until I meet a gruff orc who makes me dream about a future by his side.

Alwen

A year ago, one of the males in my village hurt me. When he tried to do it a second time, I took care of that problem —permanently. Then I'm selected for the annual Monster Mate Hunt where two village women must enter the forest to be claimed as an orc's bride. If an orc tries to take me, I'll handle him just as I did the man in my village.

To my dismay, I'm captured by a band of treacherous thieves. I'm planning my escape when an enormous, snarly orc attacks the camp. He slays the thieves and announces I'm his fated mate.

I won't go down without a fight. If only I didn't swoon whenever he comes near.

Zickar

I have one purpose: to find my brother, Dakur, and bring him back to our clan. When the path leads me to Alwen, she sparks my clan pendant, proving she's mine. She fights me at every turn, and I can tell she was hurt in the past. This pretty maiden deserves to be treated gently, and I'm just the male to do it. In no time, I can't imagine a life without her.

But when someone steals her from me, I'll cross the ends of the continent to save her. Alwen's my fated mate, and I'll do anything to make her mine.

Orc's Maiden is Book 3 in the Monster Mate Hunt Series. Expect a seductive orc hero with a creative . . . (cough), size difference, a fierce, wounded woman who softens only for him, plus a fantasy world you'll want to live in. HEA guaranteed. Each book is standalone, but the series is more fun if read in order.

Trigger: references to a prior assault—not shown on the page.

Monster Mate Hunt

Books in Order:

Orc's Mate

(a prequel novel –

FREE with newsletter sign-up)

Orc's Craving

Orc's Fate

Orc's Maiden

Orc's Captive

Orc's Taming

CHAPTER I
ALWEN

Tonight, my fellow villagers expected me to leave the dubious safety of our high fortress walls and enter the forest where a big, snarly orc would fling me to the ground and claim me as his bride.

I'd been "claimed" once already—though not by an orc—and I had no interest in allowing something like that to happen again.

"It's time to leave." My mother stood stoically near the door of our tidy home beside my two sisters and brother. They all watched me. As the eldest, I'd helped raise them after our father died. And now, as the eldest, I'd take my place among those who'd been sent into the forest for the Monster Mate Hunt.

"Be strong," my mother said fiercely, her words echoed by my siblings. She bit back her sob with a knuckle pressed against her lips, but tears filled her eyes.

She knew what I'd face. She knew what had happened before. She'd helped me bury the one who'd done it.

"I'll miss you so much." I hugged her, trying not to cry. I must remain strong—as always. They'd relied on that strength for years, and in this, I'd show them I could face anything. I'd leave the village fortress with my chin held high.

If I showed weakness, someone would use it against me.

I hugged each of them, sharing a bit of advice.

"Remember, when you shoot, your arm tends to pull to the right," I told my younger brother. "Then you miss."

Bredar nodded, his lower lip quivering. He was only thirteen. Much too young to have to hunt to provide for our family. But there was no one else. My sisters were even smaller than him.

"And you." I smiled as Nayleen tightened her spine. At ten, she could already create fine stitches. The best seamstress in our village had noticed and offered her an apprenticeship. Soon, she'd bring income to the family like our mother. "Keep working hard."

"I will, Alwen," she chirped, her voice still that of a child.

I turned to Creea, my nine-year-old sister. "Keep thinking about what you'd like to do with your life."

"I want to be a mom." She leaned against our mother. "But I want to be independent too." This, she'd learned from me, though I wasn't sure she completely agreed. As she grew older, she'd understand better.

It hurt that I wouldn't be here to see this, to guide them. To keep them safe.

"I'll find a way to come back to you all," I said.

They nodded, but we knew it would never happen. Only one woman sent to the hunt had returned to share her fate, and who knew if what she claimed was true? Orcs treating women gently, loving them even? I scoffed at the notion.

"I'll walk with you to the gate," my mother said. "Remain here," she told my sisters and brother.

We hugged again, and this time, we all shed tears. With them still streaming down my face, I left the only home I'd ever known for the final time. As I passed through the crowd who'd gathered along the narrow cobblestone road to pat my back, wish me well, and thank me for my sacrifice, I started to shake.

I'd done all I could to be strong after what happened a year ago. I'd proven I was a survivor.

But how would I gather enough strength to survive this?

"The women in my family have determination," my mother whispered. "We don't let anything drag us to the ground."

"Love you, Mother," I whispered.

"We're all in this together," she said with a sharp nod, her face wracked with grief. "Remember this, daughter." Her voice faded to almost nothing. "Please, please, remember this."

"I will, Mother." Like before, I could do no less. This realization made me hold my head higher. Wipe away my tears. And stride through the rest of the town with purpose.

If those watching thought I'd comply with this, they were wrong. No need to tell them that. Once they shoved me out the front gate, *I* controlled my future, not them.

"Remember." Mother hugged me while the guards creaked open the enormous gate. "Love you. So much. Please . . ." She pinched her eyes shut as if she couldn't bear to watch me leave her forever.

After giving her a long hug, I turned toward the gates.

The fortress had been built ages ago to protect us from the vicious shaydes who hunted at night with us their prey. It was only when a treaty was formed with the orcs eleven years ago that our destinies had changed. In exchange for their protection from the shaydes, we'd agreed to send two women out into the forest each year to be claimed as orc brides.

Actually, *we* hadn't agreed. Our men had, and they weren't the ones who had to pay the price.

Lyneth, a widow from our village and the other woman chosen for the hunt this year, stopped beside me, her stark gaze meeting mine.

"Shall we walk together?" Lyneth asked, and I

nodded. I had no intention of *walking*, but there was no harm in facing this part of the hunt together.

"Your bag," my mother said, rushing forward to hand one to me. The villagers prepared them for the women, and while I had no use for the skirt inside, I'd welcome the shirts and whatever food they'd tucked in at the last minute.

Lyneth and I slipped through the crack in the gate, hurrying across the long stretch of wavering grass between the village and the forest. I tried to remain stoic, to show those watching I didn't fear what would come next. But my hands trembled, the only thing that might give me away.

"Stay close with me, and you might just survive this," I said softly. I pulled the knife I kept sheathed at my side. "I have a weapon, and I'm not afraid to use it."

A chitter echoed from the forest ahead. A shayde hunted, but I was determined to be *no one's* prey tonight.

However, it was a toss-up whether we'd be killed by one of them or be forced to lie beneath a rutting orc. I shuddered at the thought and blocked out the memory of what happened.

Swallowing hard, I entered the woods ahead of Lyneth, my gaze seeking movement. I'd slash out with my blade if anything came near.

Guttural cries rang out somewhere in the distance, and my heart froze.

"Stay with me," I said. "Don't fall behind." I bolted into the woods, my pants legs swishing together much too loudly as I ran. I'd stopped wearing skirts a year ago, because they gave men easy access to my body.

I'd already mapped my escape out with a plan to run in the opposite direction of where I'd heard a large orc population lived. Maybe then, I'd be able to avoid the orcs seeking a bride. Pivoting, I started to tell Lyneth what we needed to do.

She was no longer behind me.

AFTER CIRCLING BACK but not finding Lyneth, I paused much too long to listen. Finally, I had to accept she was gone. I'd never find her. Remaining here would only see me captured as well.

Turning, I bolted down a thread of a trail.

I ran on and off for three days.

On the fourth, when I'd crouched down beside the river to refill my flask, a raggedy band of men snuck up behind me and grabbed me. They ripped my blade from my waist, and one of them tossed me over his shoulder. I shrieked and flailed, but I couldn't get free.

They took me to their camp and bound my hands behind my back, securing me to a tree. While they argued about what they'd do with me, the fourth of their group, a male twice my size who appeared to be made of stone, watched.

He creaked when he strode over to stand looking down at me, and while he didn't speak, he appeared willing to do whatever the men asked him. I began to suspect stone man had very little will of his own.

My gaze was drawn to a big wooden cart parked along one side of the small field surrounded by woods. Part of the cart had been covered with bars, and someone lay unmoving on the floor of the cage. A glance around showed no beast tethered who'd pull the cart, however. Maybe the enormous stone man did it for them.

"Put her in with the orc," one of the men with long, stringy dark hair hissed, his sharp gaze shooting to the big, unmoving lump inside the cage.

"*He* won't care," another said, shifting the waistband of his pants. He wore a shirt in a bright purple color unlike anything I'd seen before. "But *I* will."

The third, a bald man, snarled. "Don't touch her. She'll be worth more to us with her maidenhead intact."

Sadly, that was taken from me a year ago, and there was no reclaiming it now.

"Stay away from her. We're going to sell her," Stringy Hair said, suggesting he was the leader.

The others nodded at his words, though stone man just stared toward the fire crackling in the stone ring.

The leader's sharp eyes scanned the open meadow. He tossed a stick of wood on the fire and sparks flew into the night sky. "Keep watch on her to make sure she doesn't get away. We'll take her with the orc to the next town, where we'll fetch a good price for them both. Then we'll get rooms at an inn and pay for what we won't be claiming from her." With that, he pivoted and walked over to a hunk of meat dangling from a tree on the opposite side of the clearing. He sliced a chunk of flesh off, speared it with a stick, and returned to roast it over the fire.

My belly snarled. The bag they ignored by the river had originally held a nice sandwich made of bread and cheese, but while I'd rationed it, it was long gone. Since then, I'd eaten berries and roots quickly dug beside the river and eaten raw, but not much of anything else. Hunting was much easier when you didn't have to run all the time and had the appropriate weapons. There'd been no time to stop to lay snares, not if I hoped to avoid both the shaydes, ashenclaws, and orcs.

"The orc doesn't look healthy enough to sell," the bald man said. Taking a stick, he went over and poked the lump lying in the back of the cart. "Hey. Wake up." He gouged the stick again. "I said . . . Damn." He shot a wide-eyed gaze over his shoulder. "I think he's dead."

"He can't be," the leader said.

"If you hadn't hit him so hard in the head, he might still be alive," the bald guy snarled.

"*You* whacked him too."

"We all did, all except him." He nudged the stone man who stared down stoically but didn't shift away. "Orcs are enormous brutes. He would've killed us if we hadn't knocked him down but good."

The leader walked over to peer into the cage. "Orc skulls must not be as thick as I thought. You," he pointed to the one in the purple shirt, "climb in there and see if he's still alive or just faking it."

"Me?" Purple Shirt said. "He'll kill me."

"I promise to bury you, then," the leader said dryly. "Do it."

At his bark, Purple Shirt sidled over to the cart.

"He'd better be alive," the leader said. "They pay a good price for orcs in Feyalon, but they pay nothing for corpses."

I'd only vaguely heard of the city perched on the edge of the desert.

It didn't take long for the guy in purple to determine the orc was dead. Snarling, the three men made the stone man dig a hole at the edge of the meadow and dump the body inside, covering him and packing down the dirt.

"We can't stay here," the leader said. "The corpse will draw shaydes and ashenclaws."

They put out the fire and packed their things in the open part of the cart. I was tossed into the now-empty cage and when I tested the door, I found it locked. Only the green orc blood stain on the wooden floorboards kept me company.

The stone man hefted the front of the cart and started pulling it down a rough trail weaving through the woods. He kept going through the night and all the next day with seemingly no effort, only stopping at dusk when the leader shouted "halt." They'd chosen another meadow for their resting place.

"We'll sleep here tonight," the leader said. The others

unpacked the cart and dumped me on the ground near a new fire, securing my hands to a tree behind me.

My belly grumbled when they started cooking meat again. The guy with the purple shirt untied one of my hands and gave me a hunk. I ripped through it, eating it fast before staring at the haunch with endless hunger.

The leader came around and stooped down behind me to retie my hands, but he paused, his head jerking up and his gaze fixed on the woods on the opposite side of the meadow.

A chitter erupted from that direction—a shayde coming too close?

I scrunched down on the ground. If they ran, I'd be pinned here as prey.

Freezing, the guys stared in that direction. Even stone man looked that way.

A shayde ran into the clearing with an orc brandishing two long blades riding on its back.

Stone man bolted in the opposite direction, disappearing into the forest.

The leader strode out into the clearing, his long knife drawn, and barked out a challenge.

Foolish man. We'd established a treaty with the orcs because they were so much stronger than us.

As the orc leaped off the shayde's back, the snarling beast pounced on the leader, dragging him to the ground. The beast shredded through the leader's throat in seconds.

Gulping, I turned away, not having the belly to watch what happened next.

Purple Shirt and the bald guy fled into the woods where the stone man had disappeared.

The orc didn't give chase.

"Off," he said to the shayde, nudging the creature away from the dead leader with a tap of his knee. I expected the beast to kill the orc, but instead, it only sat on its haunches, looked up at him, and purred.

Until its gaze shot to the cage. It trotted over and sniffed. Then it tipped back its head and wailed.

A long sigh slipped from the orc, and he bowed his head, his weapons slumping at his sides. He sheathed one and clutched the sun-shaped pendant he wore on a strip of leather around his neck. "To the wind, the sea, and the mighty trees in the forest, I send your spirit. Dakur, my friend and caedos. You will be greatly missed."

"The orc was called Dakur?" I asked, struggling to rise to my feet. If I was going to die tied to a tree and from a blow from this male's blade, I'd do so while standing.

His head snapped my way. "You saw what happened?"

I shrugged. "He was dead a few days ago. They said they hit his head a bunch of times while capturing him. When they caught me and brought me to their camp, he was lying in the cage, not moving. They poked and prodded him, but he was already dead. They buried him."

"Where?" he barked.

"In a meadow a few days' travel from here. I'm not sure I could take you there, however." And why would I? The orc was buried, which was a better ending than the one I would soon face.

"Remain here," he snarled. With his weapons drawn, he leaped onto the shayde and urged it into the forest where the men had run.

"Sure," I whispered. "I'll just stay here. Think about leaving a knife, why don't you? Then I can cut myself free and run as far from here as possible."

There were no knives in sight, unfortunately, and there wasn't enough length on my rope to reach where the leader had fallen to snag his blade.

I pressed my back against the tree and waited, unsure what would happen next. The orc would've killed me already if he planned to do so, correct?

I wasn't sure what he would do when he got back, but the hollowed out feeling in my belly suggested all sorts of horrible things.

"Don't think about it," I hissed. "Think about escaping this trap as soon as you can." With a pert nod, I sat on the ground once more, staring into the fire.

Hoarse cries rang out in the distance, one after another, and quickly silenced.

A short time later, the orc melted from the woods without the shayde. Chitters far in the distance suggested . . . Bile roared up into my throat, but I forced it back down. It was better not to think about what the shayde might be doing to the bodies.

The orc stooped down and wiped blood off his blades in the deep grass. He sheathed the weapons and strode over to stand in front of me, big, brawny, and much too intimidating.

When he pulled a short knife from his waistband, I flinched, though he didn't appear to notice. Instead, he stared down at the underside of his left arm.

"Dakur was my brother," he said softly. "When my parents were killed by ashenclaws, his mother raised me as if I was her own. Dakur was a year older than me, and from then on, I loved him like a brother. He was the best of our clan, the wisest and most savvy caedos we've had for many generations. No one will ever be able to replace him in my heart."

With a grunt, he slashed a line in his arm, whispering. "Dakur. May you dance among the stars forever."

My throat tightened, though I wasn't sure why. I hadn't known the dead orc, yet I felt as if I should mourn his loss too.

"I'm Zickar," he said, cleaning his knife and returning it to the sheath secured to his loincloth. Green blood trickled down his arm, but he didn't seem to care about cleaning it up.

"I'm Alwen."

"I'm not sure what I should do with—" His words choked off, and a shudder ripped through him.

As if a star had shot down from above and hit it, Zickar's pendant blazed. The light was so bright, I had to shield my eyes.

Zickar gasped. I would too if that happened to me.

He stalked closer to me and tipped my face up with gentle fingertips on my chin, tipping it this way and that to study it. His heavy gaze slide across my body with an intensity that made electricity shoot down my spine.

I was decent sized for a woman and muscled from my years of hunting, but this male towered over me, almost twice my height and width. There didn't appear to be a scrap of fat on his muscle-bound body.

He wore nothing but a loincloth, and I couldn't stop myself from gaping at his broad shoulders, his narrow waist, and the big bulge shifting beneath the cloth bound around his waist.

He took my arm in a tight grip and stared down into my eyes with an intensity that rocked me to my core. "I, Zickar, claim you in the name of the Matis Clan."

His words were enough to shake me out of my uncomfortable perusal of his gorgeous—no, he was *ugly*—body. "You're not claiming me. I belong to myself."

He snorted. "You belong to *me*."

"Never," I vowed.

"We shall see, shall we, pretty maiden?"

CHAPTER 2
ZICKAR

This female the clan fates had chosen for me was small, slight, and ornery. She wore a simple shirt and pants like a male might, though her long hair and tiny, delicate features insisted she was female.

I didn't mind her snarls since it showed she had spirit. She'd pass that on to our orclings.

As for her size, how was I supposed to get my cock inside her? Her passage would be as tiny as her. I was average sized for an orc, but even then, I towered over her. And I was above average sized elsewhere.

Ah, well. I would find a way to plant my seed inside her, and that was all that mattered. Despite everyone stating matings chosen by our clan pendants brought true love, I didn't want that. How could I be happy when Dakur . . .

I still couldn't believe it was true. When I last saw him, he was so strong. Alive.

Staring at the infernal cart where my brother had perished, I snarled. I began pacing, unsure what I should do next.

I had no body to take back to the Matis Clan. His mother wouldn't be able to wash him, dress him, or kiss his forehead one last time before we lit his pyre.

I wanted to rip through the males once more, make them pay for what they'd done. Add another slice to my arm.

But I had a new mate to care for whether I wanted one or not. For now, I must shrug my sorrow aside and focus on her.

A caedos needed a mate and the orclings that would come from such a union. And once I'd returned to the clan, and we'd properly mourned his loss, I would have to step into his role myself. I'd never believed I'd be called to lead my clan. Dakur would always be the caedos of my heart.

I needed my friend. To laugh with, jog next to on a hunt and sit together beneath the stars to dream about our future.

I was his second, his younger brother even if not in blood, which meant everyone would expect me to lead, even our mother. Tenkaril could foretell the future. Had she seen this happen? She must've.

I gnashed my teeth and paced in front of the female who watched with a scowl on her face.

Why hadn't my mother told us? We could've stopped it from happening.

"What are you going to do with me now?" Alwen asked, and when she strained forward, grunting, I realized she was tied to the tree behind her.

Fury rose inside me. No one treated my mate in such a manner.

But I'd already made the human males pay for Dakur's death. I couldn't go back and flog them some more to get revenge for them binding my mate.

Striding over to her, I pulled my knife again. She flinched, but I ignored the gesture. She'd be wise to fear me. All her villagers did. The only reason they made the treaty with orcs was because they feared the shaydes more than us.

"I'm going to free you." I paused, narrowing my gaze on her face. "If I release you, will you run away?"

"Of course I will."

I snorted, appreciating her honesty. "Then I should keep you bound. You're staying with me, mate."

"I told you, I'm not your mate, and I'm not allowing you to claim me."

"I don't want a mate, but I need one."

Her head tilted, and she watched me as intently as I did her. "Why?"

She was pretty, I'd give her that, even if it was clear by the dirt on her face and clothing that she hadn't bathed in days. But I didn't need to answer her questions or do more than plant orclings in her body.

"I'll do my duty and rut with you before we return to my clan," I said.

"How kind of you." Sarcasm dripped from her words. She struggled to get to her feet, a challenge while bound. "I assume you'll force me." Her chin lifted, and her flinty gaze met mine. "That's what I've been told for most of my life."

"I'm no brute."

"Yet you plan to keep me tied. Mate with me against my will. I won't stand for it."

"Don't think you can disarm me, wound me, or outsmart me, pretty one."

"Fuck you."

"Soon and with pleasure."

She tried to drive her knee up, but I deflected it easily with my shin.

"Try again, mate," I said with a chuckle.

"Fuck you," she shrieked.

I grinned. "You're a mouthy thing, pretty maiden. I'll give you that." My gaze shot to her ripe lips. They were full. Puffy. What would they feel like beneath mine?

"Don't call me that."

"You're pretty. You're a maiden." I leaned close enough to catch her scent. Being so dirty, she should stink, yet she smelled like a spice I'd longed for all my life but never discovered.

She smelled like home.

I reeled away from her. My home was with my clan, not some random female my pendant seemed to think belonged to me.

"I'm not a maiden," she snarled.

"Good, then you'll know what to expect when I rut with you." I sliced through the tie connecting her to the tree and one of her wrists, wrapping the end still bound to around my palm.

She strained away from me, but I held her well. "You said you weren't going to release me."

"We need to bathe."

She looked me up and down. "You're sweaty. Bloody. *You* need to bathe, not me."

"You'll bathe along with me." I tugged her toward the river, snagging my sack as I passed it. I'd dropped it from Taen when we burst into the clearing.

Days ago, I left my clan with my fellow orc, Brec, riding a second shayde. When we came to a split in the scant trail left by whoever took Dakur, the shaydes paused. Taen wanted to go east and Noul west. Brec and I decided to separate to give Dakur the best odds of being found. When the trail went cold, Brec would return to the clan with Noul.

"What if I don't want to bathe?" Alwen asked in a normal voice I'd never use in a dark forest with predators around. "Sure, I stink, but that's a good thing. It might keep you from rutting with me."

I held up my hand.

"Yeah, I know," she snapped. "I need to stop—"

I slipped my hand over her mouth and lowered my pack to the ground so I could pull one of my long blades.

Alwen struggled for only a second before her gaze locked on the ashenclaws slinking onto the path between us and the river ahead, their gray fur gleaming in the scant moonlight.

The top of their heads came to my upper thigh, and a pack of them would prove a challenge even for a hardened orc like me.

His claws digging into the soil, the lead male snarled.

I snarled back and showed my blade. My grim smile grew. *Try me.*

They slunk back into the brush along the trail, their tails tucked between their legs.

I released Alwen, but she remained at my side, clutching the top of my loincloth.

"Why didn't they attack us?" she whispered.

"They wisely fear me."

She looked up at me. "I hunt. Maybe they were afraid of me."

"Do you think so, pretty maiden?"

A smile flittered across her plush lips, sinking back to a frown much too fast. "Probably not. I don't even have a weapon any longer. Or my bag of clothing. I have nothing. *I'm* nothing." Her sigh bled out.

"You're my mate. That's enough." Tightening my grip on the rope secured around her wrist, I moved forward, quickly passing the area where we'd seen the ashenclaws. If they were near, they remained hidden. Wise move on their part. I was angry enough I'd welcome their challenge.

When we reached the river, I pulled a tunic out of my

bag and handed it to Alwen. "You can wear this after you wash."

She held it in her outstretched hand, plucked between her finger and thumb, her nose wrinkling. "I assume it's yours."

"It's clean. I haven't worn it yet." I frowned down at her. "Do I need to tie you to a tree while I bathe, or will you promise to remain with me at least for tonight?"

"Not if you plan to rut with me."

"I'll give you a few days to get used to the idea. Then I'll rut with you."

"I'll be long gone by then."

"So you say."

She stomped one of her tiny feet. "So I'll *do*."

We'd see about that.

I was beginning to enjoy the verbal sparring between me and my mate, and I wasn't sure what to think about that.

I didn't want to like anything about this female.

But I couldn't seem to hold myself back.

CHAPTER 3
ALWEN

"Turn away while I bathe," I snapped.

He unsheathed his weapons, dropping the two long blades and the shorter one on the shore. With a twitch of his thick green orc lips, he released the tie on his loincloth. His gaze remained locked with mine while he slowly unwound it.

Heat climbed into my cheeks, and my body trembled. I was frightened about what he would soon do, that was the only reason I felt as if something inside of me was softening.

No! The last thing I'd ever do was soften toward this orc. I didn't like him. I wanted to escape him. And I definitely didn't want to see what he hid beneath his loincloth.

Yet I kept watching, daring him, I supposed.

He tugged the last bit of cloth away from his body and stood with it dangling from his hand.

His cock was big, thick, and as green as the rest of his body. It was long, too, and as I gaped at it, it twitched, coming alive.

If I wasn't mistaken, he had a smaller cock mounted above the first. I had to be imagining such a thing, however. No one had two cocks.

I swallowed, but the lump of fear in my throat wouldn't go down. "Don't come near me," I snapped, backing away as far as the rope would allow. "I mean it. I'll kick you. Gut you. Scream."

He frowned, his head tilting. "I told you I wouldn't touch you."

"Not yet." Panic lifted my voice to a screech. "Please don't come near me!"

He blinked once. Twice. Then the lines on his face smoothed. "I won't. I promise you, pretty maiden."

"I told you I'm not a maiden." Now I really was screeching, but with fright, not anger.

"Who hurt you?" he growled, his gaze shooting about wildly. "I'll kill him."

I lifted my chin. "Turn away, and I'll bathe. I won't run—for now."

Without saying anything further, he dropped the rope and went to the edge of the river, where he stooped down and scrubbed his loincloth.

I stared at his back rippling with muscles, the greenish-gold skin nicked with scars of various ages. His ass was nicely rounded and equally muscular, as were his thick thighs. Everything about his body shouted perfection.

I'd be foolish not to admit that I found him attractive, not repulsive. I should be turning away myself, but I couldn't make myself do it.

He'd dropped the rope. Only now did it sink in. I should run, right? A promise made to a captor meant nothing.

I peered into the dark woods. We'd just seen ashen-claws on the trail. Shaydes also hunted at night. While I could climb a tree, I had no weapons to defend myself. I doubted he'd allow me to steal any of his even though they lay on the shore. They were still well within his reach. He would move fast, trap me, and then he wouldn't trust me again.

While I didn't need his trust, I'd bide my time until the right opportunity arose, and it wasn't now.

He laid his wet loincloth on a large rock to dry and kept his back to me, staring out at the river. "I'm going to swim and bathe. Do you know how to swim?"

"I do." But that didn't mean I'd do such a thing with him.

"If you wish to bathe and wash your clothing, donning my shirt after, I promise I won't look your way."

"Why not, when you plan to rut with me soon? I imagine you'll want to check out what will soon be yours." The thought snarled through me, tangling into a knot I'd never unwind.

His chest expanded, and his long sigh bled out. "I'll never force you." With that, he strode into the water, scattering droplets that gleamed in the moonlight. When the water reached his waist, he dove forward, swimming beneath the surface to emerge in the center of the slow-moving river. He didn't turn my way, and he didn't gape like the fiend who'd stolen what he shouldn't.

I wanted to call out that he might say he wouldn't force me, but that I'd never willingly lie beneath him while he rutted, but I held back the words. I did want to bathe and wash the clothing I'd worn for days. I stunk, and I didn't like it.

Turning my back to him, I quickly stripped and, with my skin aquiver, I stepped into the water, sucking in a breath at how cold it was. When the water covered my chest, I washed my clothing and laid it on the boulder near Zickar's loincloth.

By then, the water felt amazing. I dunked down and ran my fingers through my hair, scrubbing my scalp and wishing I had soap to fully wash it. When I bobbed above the surface, Zickar stood nearby.

I yelped.

He lifted his hands. "I only came near to give you the soap." With his head turned away; he held it out to me. "I've washed. You can do the same." Pivoting, he swam toward shore, stepping out and stooping forward to pull something from his bag. My jaw ajar, I stared at his naked ass, wishing I could find something unappealing about him. He was gruff and grumpy, and he'd made demands, but so far, he hadn't hurt me.

That didn't mean he wouldn't.

CHAPTER 4
ZICKAR

Fury churned through me, although I kept my face neutral.

If Alwen was already safe with my clan, I'd go to the human village and slay the male who'd harmed her. I'd stab him through, burn him alive, then stomp on his carcass for what he'd done.

And I didn't even know his name.

Keeping my gaze lowered, I sat on a boulder while she swam and washed.

"I was walking home after work one night when he grabbed me," she whispered, her light voice floating across the water like mist.

"Who is he?" I growled. "What's his name?"

"I struggled. I mean, I'm strong!" Her voice cracked. "Pretty strong for my size. I've hunted for my family since my father died. I provided meat, herbs, and roots for my growing siblings and mother. In addition to that, I worked for the butcher, a job that might turn many stomachs but gave us coin to buy the things I couldn't gather in the woods."

"What is his name?" I snapped.

"But I wasn't strong enough to get away. Not strong enough to make him stop." She dragged in a breath and shot the words out with her exhale. "But when he tried again, I stabbed him." Her low laugh rang out. "That slowed him down very nicely."

"What is his name?" I roared.

"It no longer matters. He died from the wound I gave him, and Mother and I took care of the body. So in this, I won. *I* defeated the threat. *I* kept him from doing that to me or anyone else again."

I lifted my head to find a feral grin on her face. With her hair slicked back wet, and her lashes glistening with water, she was the prettiest sight I'd ever seen.

Desire rose inside me, not to take this mate or claim her, but to win the fearsome heart of this brave warrior.

"I'd kill him if he wasn't already dead," I said.

"I appreciate that." She turned and swam upriver, her strokes strong and sure.

What would it be like to have this female want me, to offer herself to me? Would I be able to show her that pleasure, not pain, could be found with another?

I wanted to be the male she discovered this with.

"I will not rut with you," I said when she turned to swim back in my direction.

She paused, treading water. "Not for a day or so, you said."

"Not *ever* unless you ask me to. But I do want you to return to my clan with me." I held up my hand when her face tightened. "You'll be safe there. No one will harm you, and you can live among us without fear. I'll make sure you have all you need. A home all of your own, plenty of food to eat, and the kindness of those around you."

I'd battle anyone else who tried to claim her, but such was the way of my clan. My pendant wouldn't be the only one to burst into flames when she came near.

So be it.

"Why would you do this?" she asked. "As you said, your clan pendant has chosen me as your mate."

"Because you've been wounded, and you need time to heal."

"What if I heal and . . . want someone other than you?"

"You are free to claim whoever you please."

I had no idea how, but she'd touched my heart already, and the last thing I'd ever do was show her that all males took what they wanted by force.

"Can I think about your offer?" she asked, nibbling on her lower lip.

"Do you have any true choice?" I couldn't keep the edge from my voice. If she thought I'd leave her here in the forest where horrible things might happen to her, she was wrong. I might never be able to claim her as my own, but I'd die to protect her.

Her lips curled up on one side. "Not yet, but who knows what might happen by morning?"

Shaking off my unreasonable jealousy, I stood and wrapped the damp loincloth around my body. It would rub, but she didn't need to see my semi-stiff cock that insisted I needed to take her right this instant.

I leaped from one boulder to another, grabbing her clothing as I passed. Landing on the shore, I strapped on my weapons and lifted the drying cloth I'd taken from my bag. Since I could hear her splashing through the water, approaching me, I draped the cloth over my shoulder, not turning to face her.

"Use this to dry. I'll give you time to dress." I nudged my tunic her way with my foot.

"I'm sure you pity me," she said as she dragged the cloth off my shoulder. A rustle told me she was rubbing her body.

"I *respect* you."

"And you didn't before?" She huffed. "All it took was me telling you about my past? If I'd known, I would've done it the second we met."

"Are you hungry?"

"Nice change of subject, and yes. The men didn't feel compelled to feed me more than once."

A growl ripped through me, and I wished one of them was here so I could lift him off his feet by his neck and shake him. I wasn't usually a violent person; I'd never hit someone, and I rarely snarled. But the thought of anyone causing Alwen pain made my muscles quiver and my heart thump like a furious beast in my chest.

"I've got food in my bag," I said.

"Will we remain here tonight?"

"Taen will come to me soon, and we'll ride her until we reach my clan."

"I assume Taen is the shayde you rode into the meadow." Her voice shook. "I have no idea how that's possible. Shaydes are predators. Creatures that will happily rip us apart."

"Dakur . . ." I pinched my eyes shut for a moment before opening them. "Dakur found three of them when they were kits and raised them with our clan. They're tame. Pets."

"I see." Clothing rustled as she dressed, and she actually braced her hand on my back while she donned her shoes. It felt good having her do this, good to help her in this tiny way. "How long will it take to reach your clan?"

"Walking? Four days. On Taen? Only two."

"I assume we'll sleep during the day."

"You can sleep while I guide Taen at night as well. I'll hold you."

"I'll have to think about that." She walked around to stand beside me, and I gaped to see her wearing my shirt and possibly nothing else.

My cock stirred again, but I suppressed it, something I suspected I was going to have to do quite a bit until I showed this female—my clan-chosen mate—that I was the male she could love for a lifetime.

No longer did I see her as a female to give me orclings. Yes, I wanted children, but Alwen was much more than that.

She'd touched me when no one else ever had except perhaps Dakur and Tenkaril, though they were family.

"Let's walk to the camp," I said gruffly, tightening my grip on one of my blades. Since I didn't sense anything dangerous near, I left the others sheathed.

"Thank you."

"For what?"

"Even if pity's your motivation, I'm grateful you're not going to make me do anything I don't want to."

"I have infinite patience." It was time for me to start using it.

"You sound like you think my feelings toward you might change."

They should, if the history of true mates was anything to go by. Each fell deeply for the other—and fast. But I wouldn't tell her that, because I suspected she'd rightly view that as another form of force.

"If they do, be sure to tell me," I said lightly, shooting her a smile.

She grunted. "Don't start dreaming about a future with me where I'll greet you each night with open arms."

Sadly enough, I already did.

CHAPTER 5
ALWEN

I'd happily take pity from this male over a determination to rut with me.

I walked beside Zickar back to the camp, pausing when he did, while we were still in the woods. Through the trees, I could see the fire flickering in the ring and the empty cage.

Zickar stared down at the ground, but nothing appeared amiss there to me.

"Wait here," he hissed, moving forward.

I slunk close to a tree, pressing my back against it.

Zickar froze. His head cocked, and he drew his second blade from its sheath at his side. Finally, he walked out into the clearing and paced around, studying the ground, before reentering the woods, moving nearly silently.

This male was a hunter like me.

Within moments, he returned to my side and nodded for me to follow him into the clearing.

"What's wrong?" I whispered, my skin prickling with fear.

He shrugged. "It's probably nothing." He studied the area for a long while again before his shoulders loosened.

The shayde hadn't returned, but maybe it was lounging somewhere in the woods.

Zickar must've thought something similar, because he called its name. When it didn't bound into the meadow, he lifted his pendant and blew across it, creating a low, mournful sound. Waiting, he continued to frown.

"Where's your . . . shayde?" I asked, surprised anyone would name a creature that would happily kill us.

"Taen always comes to my call."

"Do you think it was harmed or something like that?"

He shrugged. "I'm not sure. If he hasn't returned by morning, I'll look for him."

While I remained here alone? A shiver shot through me. Funny how I'd hoped for a stray moment where I could run away, only to find myself wanting to cling to this big burly orc for protection.

"I can collect wood for the fire," I said.

"Eat first." Sitting by the fire, he pulled a wrapped pack from his bag and opened it on his palm, revealing chunks of what looked like grain and berries stuck together with something that glistened in the moonlight. As I settled on the ground near him, he handed me a chunk and ate another.

My belly had hollowed out so much, I'd happily eat

grass. The bar tasted amazing, and I gobbled it down, gazing longingly at the rest.

He studied them as well before handing me a second, though he didn't take another for himself.

"I can't eat more than you," I said, holding it toward him.

"Why not?"

"You're almost twice my size. You need more than me."

"I've eaten recently. You have not." He grunted. "Eat it. We don't want you passing out from hunger."

"Ah, yes. I might need to run from ashenclaws or shaydes who are not part of your pack." A bit of rancor came through in my voice, but I didn't mean much by it. I was grateful he was offering me his protection, though I wasn't sure I wanted to travel with him to his clan. Live with orcs? Everyone in the village would be scandalized.

Although everyone in the village had been quite happy to shove me through the fortress gate as an offering to the orcs in exchange for their protection. Would anyone other than my mother and siblings think about me fondly again? Sadly, no. They'd gladly taken what I brought back from foraging and a hunt, but they hadn't cared one bit about the person providing it.

"Yes, ashenclaws," he said. "As for wood, we don't need any."

"A fire will keep shaydes and other threats away for the rest of the night."

"We won't remain here in the meadow."

"I thought we weren't leaving until your shayde reappeared?"

"We won't, but we'll sleep in a tree."

I tipped my head back, studying the trees surrounding the meadow. "How will we sleep up there?"

"You'll see. Do you need to visit the woods or anything like that before we climb?" He took my wet clothing and draped it on tree branches to dry, reminding me of how little I wore. His tunic was huge, gaping at the top enough to almost reveal my breasts, though the hem hung beyond my knees. I wore nothing underneath, and the thought of being exposed like this made my skin crawl. But he'd assured me he wouldn't touch me until I wished for such a thing, and I was going to believe him for now.

While most males couldn't be trusted, I sensed Zickar could be, though I had no idea why. Maybe it was the steadfast resolve coming through in his voice when he spoke, or the integrity in his dark eyes.

I'd learned quickly how to judge those who came near me.

"I don't need the woods," I said, knowing what he meant.

"All right, then." He strode into the forest, and I followed, not sure how this would work out. Would he boost me up into a tree and find another for himself, or—

He stopped and gazed up at a tree so wide, it would take many arm spans to encircle it. Before I could utter even a peep, he'd grabbed me around the waist and tossed me up. "Grab the branch and pull yourself onto the top."

I wrapped my arms around it, my legs floundering, unsure I could do what he asked.

A jump, and he stood on the branch above me, gazing down with humor in his eyes.

"Need help, pretty maiden?" he asked with a shake in his voice.

"Don't laugh at me." I swung my foot up, hooked it on the branch, and used the leverage to drag myself up onto the limb on my belly.

Only as I lay there panting did I realize the tunic had ridden up to expose everything from my waist down.

CHAPTER 6
ZICKAR

My mate was lovely everywhere, but I averted my gaze when I caught her ripe ass gleaming in the moonlight.

She hastily tugged my tunic down around her thighs, a challenge while she lay on her belly, clinging to the branch.

"Ugh," she said. "You didn't see that."

"I saw nothing."

Everything.

My cock started to stiffen, but I thought of the precision needed to shoot an arrow, of how a shayde needed its hooves cleaned regularly or they could develop rot. The latter helped the most. Nothing beat thinking of hoof rot to take the energy out of a cock.

"Can I help you?" I offered, extending my hand.

She took it with a sigh and used it to get to her feet. "I'm not looking down."

"Why not?"

She shoved her hair off her face. "Doesn't everyone prefer to keep their feet on the ground?"

"You don't enjoy heights?"

Her lips trembled, and I noted how pink they were, how ripe. "Who does?"

I chuckled. "Everyone in my clan."

"It's not like I need to fly."

"Some orcs do."

A frown filled her pretty face. "They have wings? I've seen your back. You don't have them unless they're very well hidden."

"No wings, but some orcs bond with voxes, large, winged creatures. They use them to travel."

Her face cleared. "That must be how they—*you*—travel across such vast distances. Although, it appears you travel on shaydes as well."

"Just the three Dakur adopted and raised." Where was Taen? He should be here by now. He wouldn't run wild and abandon me. We were clan.

"Do those in your clan fly with voxes?"

"We do not."

"Fair enough." She grunted and looked around. "We're going to sleep here?"

"We haven't climbed high enough to be safe yet."

"Your shayde won't protect us?"

"He would if he was here, but he isn't. I'm confident he'll return by morning."

"And if he doesn't?"

"I'll deal with that situation then. Come. Let's keep climbing." I reached for her waist again.

Her hands lifted, and she backed against the trunk. "I'll climb by myself. Maybe then, I'll do so in a more dignified manner."

"I don't mind the view."

Her lips thinned. "I'm sure you don't."

"You have a lovely body. It's my honor to appreciate it."

"That's sweet and all, but it's time to climb." She peered up, but I'd already looked. The closest branch was well out of her reach. Glaring at me, she stomped her foot. "You picked this tree on purpose."

"What do you mean by that, mate?"

"You knew I wouldn't be able to climb this one by myself."

"I picked it because it's big and the branch where we'll shelter tonight is wide enough not only to support our weight, but we also probably won't roll off."

"Ugh," she said again. "I don't want to think of falling." Peering at the ground, she shuddered and latched onto the tree trunk. "I'm not sure I can bear to be much higher off the ground."

"You could close your eyes."

Her head tilted, and she frowned. "Do you think that'll help?"

"It never hurts to try."

She heaved a sigh. "You'll have to help me, then."

I'd suspected I'd have to already and not only

because of her apparent fear of heights. What kind of caedos mate would she make if she was afraid to ascend to where we lived?

I'd begun to suspect she'd be the best kind. I was grateful for the gift the clan fates had given me even if it would take time before she wished to be with me.

She would get where she needed to be regarding me, however. I was confident of that and not only because I'd do my best to charm her, but because the fates wouldn't have given her to me if we wouldn't love each other for a lifetime.

"Would you like to ride on my shoulder or in my arms, pretty maiden?"

Her fear of heights temporarily forgotten; she placed her fists on her hips. "I see you persist in calling me that despite me telling you it's not factual."

"You're pretty. No one will convince me otherwise." I scooped her up around her waist and lifted her to the next branch, this time making sure she was high enough she could lay across the branch without having to pull herself up with her heels. "As for being a maiden, what's stolen isn't the same as what's given."

"It doesn't matter how it was taken. The fact remains that I'm no maiden."

"Does it make you sad or feel pain when I call you that?"

She moved to a sitting position, dangling her legs but clinging to the branch in front of her with both hands. "Why would it?"

I shrugged and leaped up to join her.

"You make that look so easy," she said.

"I'm bigger than you. Stronger."

"That's a fact. I'm not completely useless, however. I can hunt if you've got a bow and arrow, and I don't mind cleaning a kill. I worked for the butcher in the village, and he'll miss me as much as my family."

We slowly kept going, and I could see that talking while we did it distracted her from how high we were climbing.

"We can stop here," I finally said, sitting with my back against the tree. I patted my lap. "Time to sleep, mate."

"You expect me to sit on your thighs?"

"And my cock, but I'm going to do my best to ignore that fact."

She sucked in a breath. "You said you wouldn't push me."

"I won't, but that doesn't mean I won't tell you what to expect. When you're sitting on my lap, snuggling against my chest with my arms around you, it's only natural that my cock will respond to your presence." And the fact that she wore nothing beneath my tunic, but I wasn't mentioning that.

"You must control it." She looked at me so sternly, her gaze darting to my groin, that it was all I could do not to laugh.

"Unfortunately, it has a mind of its own."

"How is that even possible? I assumed . . ."

"What?"

"That you could control your body's response to others. That when you were ready to rut, you told it to respond, and it did."

"And when I come, I'm telling my cock it's time to do so as well?"

She shrugged. "I guess."

My mate truly was a maiden. One male forcing himself to take what he shouldn't didn't change that. I'd take things slowly and be patient. The last thing I'd ever want to do was frighten or hurt her.

Maybe she'd never feel comfortable being with me sexually, and that would be all right. My cock would complain, but her spirit was what mattered most.

"I'll sit on the branch by myself," she said, carefully lowering herself and spreading her legs around the thick branch. This, of course, created a shadowy gap between her legs where my tunic lifted. I averted my gaze before my cock caught wind of it and responded further. "I wouldn't want you to . . . rise because of my presence."

"Do you believe you'll be able to sleep there?" I asked, truly curious. I'd done so, but since I grew up living in the canopy, I had an innate sense of my body's position in relation to everything around me. I also had been known to tie myself to a branch just in case, though not since I was young.

"I don't expect either of us will get much sleep."

I tipped my head back against the trunk and closed my eyes. "I imagine I'll sleep well enough." Better if I held her in my arms. She was my mate, and it was hard not to feel irritated that the fates had given me someone who might never want to be with me fully.

I had to trust they had a reason, and it would show itself to me eventually.

She shifted around, hissing here and there and sighing a lot. A few gasps were followed by her smacking her palms or feet onto the branch.

Finally, I cracked one eye open, peering in her direction. "I promise not to grope you."

"What does that mean?" she snapped, sitting up and swinging her legs over the branch on either side, again giving me a nice view between them.

I struggled not to groan. "It means if you sit with me, I'll hold you. I won't touch you anywhere other than where necessary—unless you ask me to, of course."

"Which I won't."

"You've made yourself clear," I huffed. "In my arms, you'll feel safe and can rest."

"Feel safe in a male's arms? That's a switch."

"We're not all the same person." I would remain patient with her for as long as I could. "I'm not him."

"I'm sorry." She swallowed hard. "I see that's true already. I shouldn't blame every male for the actions of one."

"If I hold you in my arms, I won't have to worry about you falling off the branch."

"I don't think I'll fall."

"As long as you remain awake through the night."

She grumbled and looked around as if a better solution would present itself. "I still don't understand why we can't sleep by the fire."

"Ashenclaws aren't always afraid of it."

A shudder ripped through her. "They didn't come near while I was traveling with the men or when I was alone. I thought the fires . . ."

"There were five people in your camp, including you. I imagine that many was a big enough deterrent. But if one of you had strayed away from the group . . ."

"You're saying they were near all the time."

"I suspect so. They enjoy an easy meal, and people traveling through their territory sometimes present one."

"All right," she sighed. She got onto her hands and knees and crawled toward me, wincing when the bark bit into her skin. When she reached me, she paused, looking up at me. "I'm not sure how to sit on you."

I had one good suggestion that I wouldn't name.

I lifted her and held her in front of me easily. "Spread your legs."

Color flooded her face. "I'm not wearing anything under your tunic," she whispered as if she worried someone would overhear.

"I'm well aware of this."

"And you've behaved like a perfect gentle-orc despite that. I appreciate your restraint."

She'd never know how tempting she was, how hard it was not to stroke the smooth skin of her thighs, to touch her face. Or how much I wanted to kiss her.

My pendant flared, reminding me again that she was the one chosen for me by the fates.

"Spread your legs and let me settle you on my lap," I croaked. "Then we can both get some sleep." Though it was killing me, I kept my smile friendly. Would she notice my hard-on?

She did as I asked, and I lowered her onto my mid-thighs to avoid her noting what I couldn't control.

"Why does your pendant keep shining?" she asked, holding her hand up to shield her eyes.

Because I haven't fucked you yet. I couldn't tell her that. "It does it randomly."

"That must make it a challenge when you hunt." Looking up at me, she yawned. "Do you think we can be friends?"

"What do you mean?"

"At first, at least. I . . . you seem nice. Sweet, even. I trust you, something I haven't done with a male outside my brother and father. I've never had a male friend, and I think it would be good to start that way."

I nodded, understanding what she was saying. "Of course."

"Thank you."

And with that, she settled against my chest and closed her eyes, her arms going partway around me.

CHAPTER 7
ALWEN

Zickar was so warm. I felt safe in his embrace, something I'd never imagined I'd feel with a male. He was a good person. Kind. Even gentle.

And despite telling myself we would only be friends, I liked him as more than a friend. I didn't know what could come from such a feeling, but for the first time since that man hurt me, I was going to let life take me wherever it pleased. I wouldn't try to control this, which was frightening in itself.

After it happened, I'd found myself again by controlling everyone and everything around me. Handing even a bit of that over to someone new was scary.

But I sensed Zickar wouldn't betray me. Maybe I was foolish to trust him so easily, but it felt right.

As dawn cracked open the sky and let in the light, I woke. Warmth surrounded me. Zickar surrounded me. I snuggled closer, savoring how wonderful it felt to feel safe.

I looked up and found him staring down at me.

"Did you sleep too?" I croaked. I felt as if I'd slumbered for hours in my safe little bed back in the village.

"Enough." His gaze drifted to my mouth, and I wondered what it would be like to kiss someone who wasn't trying to take something I wasn't prepared to give.

One of his arms left the back of my waist. He stroked his knuckles down my cheek and neck, stopping when he reached the top of his tunic.

His head curled forward, and my heart tripped over itself. For the first time since before it happened, I felt awash with desire. I wanted to feel his lips on mine. Would he kiss me softly or press down hard?

When he brought his head closer to mine, he waited again, only whispering my name. If we kissed—if we ever did *anything*—I would have to show him I wanted it.

How freeing.

I hadn't kissed anyone in over a year because I worried he'd take such a gesture as permission to do whatever he wanted with my body.

"Zickar," I breathed, my pulse soaring in my throat. I traced my fingertips up his chest and around to the back of his neck. Because I couldn't resist, I ran them through his long hair. It was softer and thicker than it appeared. I coiled some around my fingers and pressed against his neck, bringing his face close enough I could reach him.

Then I kissed him.

He froze, and for a moment, I worried this meant he didn't wish to kiss *me.* But then he groaned and pulled me tight against his chest. His mouth moved softly on mine, tentative at first, but when I gasped, nearly overwhelmed with feelings I'd never expected to have for anyone, he deepened the kiss. His tongue stroked across my lips, and I opened my mouth to let him inside. Our tongues glided together, and feelings I'd never imagined rushed through me.

I wanted this orc when I'd never wanted another.

There wasn't anything I needed more than to keep kissing him, yet I wrenched my mouth away from his. I had to think about what this kiss meant.

"You're such a brave female," he murmured, his voice mesmerizing. "I admire you very much."

Surely, he didn't bring this up because I'd kissed him. "Why?"

"Because you haven't given up. I don't just refer to you snapping at me all the time."

I flashed a smile his way. "I don't *always* snap."

"Despite being small and puny, you stick up for yourself. You're willing to fight if need be."

"Will you give me one of your knives? I feel defenseless without one."

"I'll protect you."

"You know what I mean. With a weapon, I'll feel as if I truly can protect myself. I've worn one—even to bed —since..."

"When we reach the ground, I'll give you a blade."

"Thank you. Today, we'll ride on your shayde?" I was tempted to look down, to see if the creature lurked below, but I didn't dare. Heights had always frightened me, though I had no reason for this feeling. I'd never fallen.

"We will."

"Then let's descend, shall we?" When he grinned, my heart flopped around again.

"All right." I eased off his lap and using his chest and shoulders for stability, I rose to my feet. "How are we going to get there?"

"I'll help you. Know I'll keep you safe in this as much as I did last night while you slept."

"You're going to make an amazing friend, Zickar."

A touch of sadness crossed his face before he smoothed it away. "Thank you."

He lowered me by holding onto my hands, one branch at a time, and it wasn't long before I stood on the ground beside him. He looked around, but he'd already paused a few branches up to make sure nothing predatory was near before he brought us the rest of the way down. I liked how careful he was.

"You can have this." Bending forward, he removed a sheath holding a knife from his right calf. "I'll help you put it on once you've dressed in your clothing. As much as I love seeing you wearing my tunic, you'll be more comfortable in your pants and shirt."

"You just want your tunic back," I teased as we walked side by side toward the clearing.

"It *is* my favorite shirt."

"And yet you're only wearing a loincloth."

He snorted. "I like wearing loincloths."

Of course he did.

"I was part of the Mate Hunt," I said. "My village selected me and another woman for this year's hunt. When I reached the woods, I encouraged her to run with me, but I lost her in the darkness. I looked for her but when hoots rang out, I suspected she'd already been captured, that someone was now hunting me. I bolted." I pinched my eyes shut. "I hope she's all right. I would've brought her with me if I could. Maybe then, we could've watched out for each other, and I wouldn't have been captured."

"If you weren't captured, I wouldn't have found you. I was hunting Dakur."

"I'm sorry about your friend."

"He was our clan caedos, which means leader." Zickar's voice went husky. "He'll be greatly missed."

"If it helps, I don't think he suffered. He was unconscious from the time they brought me to their camp until he died."

"I'll share this with his mother. It will bring comfort."

I felt bad for the woman who'd soon learn her son was dead.

"We can bathe quickly before we leave," Zickar said.

"Eat as well. Once we reach my clan, you'll have to share my home with me."

I understood that. He'd provide protection from the others. If his clan was as crowded as the village, I doubted they'd have an empty home to spare, especially for a solo female like me.

Before we left the woods to enter the clearing, Zickar held up his hand. A frown cratered his face as he stared toward the meadow, and I followed his gaze.

Everything appeared as we'd left it last night.

But the shayde, Taen, was nowhere in sight.

CHAPTER 8
ZICKAR

I took her hand and eased into the meadow with her so close behind me, our skin brushed.

Lifting my pendant, I blew softly across it, but despite my call, Taen didn't appear. Where was he?

I wanted to call out, but something held me back. I didn't sense eyes watching, so that couldn't be it. And if there were predators near, I'd know that as well. But I'd survived this long by trusting my instincts, and I wasn't going to abandon them now.

Last night, I'd found compacted leaves where we hadn't traveled. Had someone crept close to the meadow while we weren't there? I'd barely slept, and I planned to keep my eyes wide open at all times. Safety was a relative thing, but I'd feel more secure once we were back in my clan's territory.

There, I could call vines and move more quickly

through the forest. The vegetation in this area didn't respond to my calls; I'd tried while hunting Dakur.

Turning to Alwen, I tapped my lips, and she nodded. She was clever as well as brave, and if I'd been given the choice, I couldn't have picked a better mate. Her kiss . . . I wanted to dwell on it, to wallow in the heady feeling I'd gotten from her tentative touch, but I needed to locate Taen.

"I'm going to put you up in a tree," I whispered. "Then look for Taen."

She nodded again, and we melted back into the woods, though we didn't travel far. I boosted her up onto a low branch of a good tree, then leaped up to join her. When I'd helped her up three more branches, I waited while she eased down onto the limb with her back to the trunk.

"Go," she said softly. "I'll be fine here. I promise I won't try to climb down alone."

With a grunt of acceptance, I leaped to a nearby tree and, using the momentum, let my body swing to another. I kept going until I was close to where I'd killed the males who'd murdered Dakur before dropping to the ground. Crouched, I listened. When I heard nothing of concern, I straightened and strode to where I'd left Taen with one of the carcasses. He wasn't there, but that wasn't unusual.

Moving around that area, I picked up Taen's trail on the other side and followed it for a few cliks, concerned when I saw he was moving away from my location. Stopping, I gently blew across my pendant. Then I waited, expecting him to come bounding over to me after some wild adventure that had called him away.

He didn't come. Not then and not after I'd blown three more times.

"Gone," I hissed, peering around as if I'd see him or some sort of explanation for where he might've gone. Our shaydes were incredibly loyal. They never strayed far from the clan. That was why we'd taken two of them to hunt Dakur and why I'd asked the third to take Madr and his mate, Lyneth, to the orc city. There wasn't anyone I'd trust more than our shaydes except my close friends.

I didn't find blood, and I didn't see any evidence he'd gotten into trouble. And while I'd love to keep following his trail, my mate was waiting for me.

We'd have to walk to my clan.

I could only hope that Taen would catch up with us soon.

WE WALKED ALL DAY. Shaydes hunted at night, and while ashenclaws didn't seem to have any preference about when they stalked prey, they also seemed to prefer doing so at night when visibility had diminished and they had a better chance of spooking something into a run.

Remaining near the river that would eventually take us into the Matis Clan territory, I only paused to dig roots or pick berries. Before nightfall, we came across a good place to stop. Tall, sturdy trees grew nearby, and fish jumped in the river.

After I'd scouted the area to make sure there were no immediate threats, I stopped in front of Alwen. My mate was just as lovely now as she'd been when we first started out. Earlier, she'd complained that her hair was a mess, but I liked it this way; wild and untamed. Vicious even, though I wouldn't tell her that. I didn't know much about females, though I'd been close to a few here and there while growing up, but I knew I'd never hear the end of it if I told Alwen she appeared more than capable of ripping someone apart.

Although, with Alwen, she might actually take that as a compliment.

"I'll fish if you want to collect firewood to cook my catch," I said.

She nodded and moved quietly into the woods.

"Stay close," I called out, not liking the idea of her being far from my sight.

I strode to the river and removed the bag from my back, tugging out my fishing supplies. In no time, I'd caught three fish. I quickly cleaned them while Alwen built a good-sized pile of wood for our fire. After tindering it, I let the wood burn down until we had a solid bed of coals.

I skewered the fish on green sticks and cooked our meal over the coals. Soon they sizzled, and an amazing smell filled the air. The roots Alwen had washed and laid on rocks in the coals glistened, coated in their own juices as they roasted.

I ducked into the woods on one final errand, determined to take care of it before it got dark. Returning to our camp, I hid what I'd located near the pile of wood.

Catching the scent of the roasting fish, my belly snarled.

Alwen shot me a smile. "I'm hungry too."

"You'll never go without food once we reach my clan."

She shrugged. "As I've said, I hunted for my family, though I sold much of what I killed to the butcher I worked for, keeping just enough for us. I'm not afraid of providing for myself again."

"Will your father take over this duty now that you're gone?"

"He died five years ago, leaving me, my mother, and my three siblings to make our way as best we could."

"What will they do now that you're gone? Your loss is a hardship since it sounds as if you'd become their provider."

"I taught my brother to hunt. He's small still, but he'll do all he can."

"Will he work for the butcher too?"

"I think so. I suggested he do this, and he was going to speak to the butcher. But as I said, he's young. Old enough to work, I suppose, though I wish he could remain in school instead."

"How old is he?"

"Bredar is thirteen."

Old enough to hunt, but still a child. "Is this usual for humans?"

"To quit school and work to feed a family? Unfortunately, yes."

"You mentioned sisters?"

"Nayleen and Creea are younger than my brother." A sad smile twitched at her lips upward before they smoothed. "I miss them. Worry about them. My mother too."

"We could visit them someday. See if they'd like to live with us in my clan."

"I can't imagine my mother agreeing to such a thing. She fears orcs like everyone in my village."

"Do you?"

She shrugged. "I used to. Not any longer, not since I met you."

I was pleased that I'd shown her she had nothing to fear. "You could speak with your family. Make the offer and see what they say. Everyone would do their best to make sure your family saw they had no reason to fear us."

"I don't know yet if I'll remain with your clan but thank you just the same."

I nodded, though I was determined to show her she belonged by my side. "What's your mother's name?"

"Roolina"

If Alwen let me, I'd welcome her family and make sure they had a wonderful home, plenty of food, and friends. It couldn't be any worse a life than they lived now.

She stared into the flames. "Sometimes, I hate what life does to us. It takes, takes, takes, and rarely gives. I can't be there for them when they need me most. My little sisters . . ." She lifted teary eyes my way. "They're nine and ten, and they're already, thinking about apprenticeships. They should be playing with their cloth babies, running through the streets with their friends, dreaming." Pinching her eyes shut, she sucked in a deep breath and released it. "But they'll have to grow up quickly now."

"I'm sorry."

"Thank you. One day, I'll fix this. Somehow."

How could I tell her that I could offer her and her family this and so much more? I wasn't sure Alwen would believe me. All I could do was show her how my clan lived, then mention it to her again in the future.

I'd do this just to see my mate smile.

My throat feeling crushed, I divided up the fish and roots, placing portions on flat rocks we'd washed first in the river. We ate quickly and in silence.

"Let's wash in the river," I said after.

She tugged my tunic from my bag, and I grabbed another loincloth. I'd wash this one but let it dry after swimming rather than don it like I had last night.

After I'd looped my bag on a low tree limb to keep creatures from it, we walked through the woods to the river, me with a long blade ready in case we ran into trouble. But nothing came near us, though something bolted away from us through the woods to our right.

At the river, I turned away from her and undressed while she did the same, and it made my chest loosen to see that she trusted me with this. I wasn't going to touch her in a sexual way until she made it clear she wanted it. If that time came, wonderful. If it didn't, I'd do all I could to protect her and make her feel cherished. Not all relationships needed to be physical.

"Why don't you enter the water first?" I said, keeping my gaze on the woods near the river. I held the soap her way.

She took it from me. "Thanks." Splashes soon followed. "You can turn now," she called out. "I'm covered."

I joined her in the water, though I kept distance between us. "Would you like me to wash your hair?"

"Oh, thanks, but I can get it." She lathered it up and rinsed, then swam close enough to me to hand me the bar of soap.

I cleansed myself and floated a bit.

"I'll leave the water first and make sure it's safe," I finally said.

"You're so kind." Her voice croaked, and I was grateful once more that I could show her I was different from the male who'd hurt her. A fierce protectiveness had grown inside me, and I'd rip apart anyone who threatened her.

I stepped from the water and tied on the clean loincloth, turning to face her. Her gaze didn't meet mine. It slid up and down my body, feeling almost like a caress.

Was this mere curiosity on her part, or did she feel some attraction for me?

I hoped it was the latter.

If so, what was I going to do about it?

CHAPTER 9
ALWEN

How had I been so fortunate to wind up with someone who was kind and protective, someone who didn't make demands on my body?

I couldn't stop thinking about our kiss. I'd always assumed I'd attempt a relationship with someone one day. I didn't want to be alone forever. Sex would be a part of that, and I'd planned to bear what he did and put each time behind me. It was something I'd suffer through to have children and someone to talk to in the evenings.

But I wasn't sure when I'd ever be ready to try such a thing.

Now I had a male who claimed I was his mate. He appeared to want me unless he was correct that his cock basically had a mind of his own and randomly became erect. I couldn't imagine how awkward that could be. Imagine a part of your body making itself known when you were trying to work, relaxing, or, in this case, cleansing yourself in the water.

As we washed together and he gently left the river and made sure it was safe for me to also emerge, a feeling I couldn't define started simmering inside me. It wasn't like anything I'd felt before.

I was beginning to care for this gruff orc who treated me like a queen.

Was I attracted to my new mate?

I no longer felt fear when he was near. A warm, fuzzy feeling kept sliding through me, making my bones feel soft and melty. Every time he looked at me, my heart pattered faster than it should.

Perhaps I should consider remaining in his clan as his mate. I doubted I'd ever find another male who'd treat me with this much respect.

It might not be bad to lie beneath him when he rutted.

Something deep inside me suggested I might even enjoy it. How was that possible? Yes, I'd felt desire for males prior to that one haunting experience, but I'd thought that feeling had been stomped out of me forever.

Instead, Zickar appeared to have reignited it.

I swallowed hard while he swiped his hands across his body to remove water. I gulped when he bent over to grab his clean loincloth. And I mourned when he wrapped it around his waist, covering that part of his body.

Was desire truly growing inside me? It had felt like it during our kiss.

When he urged me to leave the water, I did so, drying quickly and dressing in his tunic that smelled vaguely like him. The coarse feel of it brushing against my naked body stimulated feelings I couldn't define.

As we walked back to where we'd left our pack, I kept thinking. And wondering. Should I do something about this feeling or suppress it?

"I have something for you," he said gruffly, walking to the stack of wood I'd collected. He lifted something the size of his fist. He held it out to me, and I stared at the wide swath of bramby brush. "Let me show you." He came around behind me and starting at the top of my head, slowly worked it through my hair, removing the snarls. "It's not the same as a wooden comb, which I'll give you when we reach my clan, but it should make your hair feel smoother."

"Thank you." My eyes kept stinging, though I wasn't sure why.

When he finished, he handed me the brush. I had no bag, so I held it, determined to take it with me when we left in the morning.

"I'll need to hunt," he said as we sat by the fire, drying and warming after our swim. "I'll fish, of course, but there's no guarantee they'll bite. I have enough berry bars for one or two days, but it'll take longer than that to reach my clan."

"I could help clean whatever you bring back to our camp."

"You mentioned hunting with a bow. When we reach my clan, I'll make you your own. Ours will be too large for you to handle. A nice, smaller one with a taut string and fleet arrows will work perfectly for you. Plus something to carry them in. Then you can hunt if you wish, though I assure you, we have plenty to eat in our clan. We all contribute as we're able, and no one ever goes to bed with a growling belly."

His clan sounded amazing. Even if I wasn't sure I'd remain with him, I was getting excited about seeing it.

"You're assuming Taen won't return to us," I said. "That we'll have to walk all the way."

"Yes, I'm preparing for more walking. If he was going to return, he would've already."

"Are you worried about him?"

"Somewhat. I can't figure out why he'd leave like that. He's loyal to a fault, and he knew I needed him."

"Maybe he found a mate?"

"That could be it."

"I hope he returns to your clan one day, then." I couldn't believe I would ever say such a thing. Worry about a shayde and wish it would come home to his clan? No one in the village would believe me.

"I'll hunt early in the morning, before the sun rises," he said, standing. He started smoothing dirt close to the fire with his foot, kicking it over the pit to put out the flames, leaving us in complete darkness. No moon shone down on us tonight, and no stars twinkled in the sky.

"I assume we'll sleep in a tree again," I said lightly, staring toward the forest that loomed around us. "I'll sleep in your lap again if that's all right."

And . . .

No, I wouldn't think about this too much. If I did, I wouldn't be brave enough to speak of it.

"Of course," he said, offering his hand to help me rise.

We packed everything, and I carefully added my brush to his bag. He hung it on a branch and, pulling one of his long blades, we ventured into the woods.

In no time, we'd found and climbed a good tree, and he'd settled against the trunk, his legs splayed around it.

Before I could weaken and remain where I was, quietly wishing him good night, I climbed onto his lap, facing him with my legs spread around his sides. His tunic rode up, but the hem still covered my thighs.

"I have something to ask of you," I croaked. Was I really going to do this?

"Whatever you please, pretty maiden."

If he kept calling me that, my heart was going to soften some more.

"Speak. I'm here to listen," he said.

"Can we kiss again?"

He sucked in a breath before his tusks flashed white in the dim light. "I'd be happy to kiss you again."

"I want to test something." Now that didn't sound

right. Here he said I was brave, but I'd soon prove I was actually a coward if I didn't make my needs known. "I enjoyed our kiss."

"Is that so?"

"It is." I nodded as if I needed body movement to reinforce my words. "And, if you're open to the idea, I'd also like you to touch my breasts."

CHAPTER 10
ZICKAR

My pendant flared, nearly blinding us both.

I clamped my hand over it, convinced I'd misheard her. She'd told me *not* to touch her breasts, something I'd ached to do while I kissed her this morning, an urge I'd keep from giving into no matter what.

"Through my shirt, of course," she hastily added.

"Of course." I stared at her, stunned. "Did you just ask me to touch your breasts while I kiss you?"

Her face darkened. Did she realize orcs had better sight in the dark than humans?

"I did." She nodded again. "See, I enjoyed the kiss, so I'd like to try that again. And because I'd also like to experiment a bit, I'd like you to touch my breasts like you would a lover."

"Why?"

"To see if that feels good too."

"And if it doesn't?"

"I'll ask you to stop. We'll go to sleep and that will be that."

If we kissed and I touched her breasts—like a lover would—I suspected I wouldn't get any sleep tonight.

"I'd be happy to touch your breasts."

"Like a lover," she insisted.

"Naturally. I'll stroke your nipples—through the cloth—and you can tell me how it feels."

My cock was on fire, standing stiff beneath my loincloth already, and we hadn't yet touched.

"Why do you wish to experiment?" I asked.

"You know I had one horrible experience."

And I'd kill the male if he wasn't dead already.

"I want children," she said softly, looking down. Did she realize her fingertips stroked across my chest, that one hand was teasing my right nipple? "To have children, I'll need to have sex. You've offered me a mating, and at first, I was resistant to the idea." She shot a look up at my face before turning her gaze downward once more. "I assumed I'd one day agree to wed a male, and I'd lie beneath him. I never believed I'd enjoy the act, but I'd bear with it to have children."

"I see." I was going to explode from her simple words. "I'll gladly give you orclings—children—if we become true mates." And I'd make for damn sure she enjoyed it. Lie beneath me while I rutted over her? Yes, at least once a night, alternating with other positions, but I'd always make sure she found her pleasure long before I gave into my own.

What she was talking about was a sexual awakening, assuming I did things right, which I would do or die trying. While it would be pure torture, I would do whatever it took to help her through both her past and the present. Because a wonderful future awaited us, and I wanted her with me when it arrived.

"*If* we become true mates," she repeated. "So will you do this for me?"

"Gladly."

"All right. I suppose I should rise on your lap to reach your mouth. You can . . . just touch my breasts when it feels like the appropriate time."

It was always the appropriate time.

I couldn't believe what I was hearing, but my heart was floundering in my chest at the thought there could be more than only friendship between us.

"I could also curl down to reach your mouth," I suggested. "Like I did this morning."

"Would that hurt your neck?"

I'd suffer gladly. "Not much."

"Let me climb on top of your lap, then."

And risk her kneeing my cock? That would hurt more than anything. "I'll curl forward," I barked.

Her fingertips froze on my chest and that was a true tragedy. "Are you upset that I asked you to do this?"

"Not in the least. This is just . . ." I could barely form words. "Unexpected."

"I'm sure you'd already resigned yourself to never touching me in this way."

"Perhaps." Not really. I was too determined and strong willed to give up that easily. I just wasn't sure how I'd be able to seduce her without betraying her trust.

"All right, then. Curl forward. We'll kiss. You'll touch my breasts—briefly, I assume, since this is a test—and I'll pull back when I've finished my experiment."

This was going to kill me, but I suspected I'd die a happy male. "When you're ready."

She nodded pertly. "Now. Let's get this out of the way so we can sleep."

Fuck sleep. I was more than ready to show my mate the pleasure that could be found between two people.

I curled my body forward until my face hovered above her upturned mouth. "Now?"

"Whenever you feel the time's appropriate. I'm not sure it'll make much difference, but I trust you enough to try."

I kissed her before she said anything further. And when she moaned and slid her hands up to grip my shoulders, I deepened the kiss, sliding my tongue into her mouth.

She bucked against me, and I truly was going to die tonight. Rather than mention that she was the one taking this further by rubbing herself against me, I did as instructed. I slid my fingertips down her neck to the top of her chest.

Then I cupped the underside of her breasts. They were large for a human, and I liked that. I couldn't wait until she asked me to suck on them—which I suspected she one day would. I'd struggle to survive until that blissful moment.

When I ran my thumbs over her nipples, they pearled, and another moan ripped through her.

My cock smacked hard against my abs, the tip thrusting through the top of my loincloth. My spur, mounted above my main shaft, quivered. If we ever connected fully, it would latch onto her clit and vibrate.

Alwen rocked against me, the juncture between her thighs hitting my cock just right.

I rolled her nipples between my fingertips, and she rubbed her groin against me faster, harder.

Our tongues dueled, stroking each other while I did the same with her nipples. She was wonderfully responsive, and I'd give just about anything to bury myself inside her. Was she wet for me already or would that take more "experimentation"? I was eager to find out. We had many days of travel ahead of us, and I was going to make the most of it.

Assuming she was ready for whatever came next.

Just when I thought I'd come, she pulled her face away. She settled in my lap, gazing up at me raptly, her mouth parted and her breaths coming fast.

"I . . ." She traced her fingers across her mouth. "Your tusks don't hurt."

"That's good." I winced, my cock throbbing with need. Would she notice if I finished it off myself? Most likely. "Do you . . ." *Get control!* I cleared my throat. "Was that acceptable to you?"

"I liked kissing you again. It made me feel all tingly inside. I wasn't afraid, not one bit."

"That's good," I bit out. "How about when I touched your breasts?"

"That felt nice."

My heart dropped all the way to the ground. "Only nice?"

"No, I mean . . ." More color flooded her face. "It felt wonderful. Why is that, do you think?"

"I believe it's natural for it to feel good. *Wonderful*, that is."

"But after what happened, I didn't expect to ever find pleasure in a male's arms."

"Perhaps having kind feelings toward the male helps?" I was flinging this stuff out there. My adopted mother would be so much better at helping Alwen through this than me.

But there was no place I'd rather be than here, discussing this with her.

"That could be it." She flashed me a smile. "I believe I like you, Zickar."

My heart pretty much exploded at her words.

CHAPTER II
ALWEN

Zickar had a hard-on, and I wasn't sure what, if anything, I should do with it. If I touched it, would that make him go wild? While it would be a challenge for him to do much of anything this high in a tree, it wouldn't take him long to take me to the ground.

No. I trusted Zickar. He wouldn't force me. He'd not only promised, but I'd also seen the goodness in his heart, and that person would never make a woman to do something like that.

Since I didn't know what to do, I decided to ignore it. I closed my eyes and rested my face against his chest.

My mind whirled, and I couldn't make it stop.

The heat of his mouth made me feel squirmy inside —in a good way. No, in a *wonderful* way. And when he'd touched my nipples? Shockwaves blasted through me, centering between my legs in that place I thought could only bring pain.

I'd rubbed against his cock, which hadn't been part of our agreement, but he hadn't complained. Or maybe his mouth and hands had occupied his mind, and he hadn't noticed.

Tomorrow, I'd ask him if I could do this again. If I felt brave, I might tell him he could put his hands beneath my shirt and touch my nipples without the cloth between them. Would it feel much different?

And if he didn't seem to notice, which I suspected he hadn't, I'd rub myself against him again. I needed to see if the feeling that grew inside me to the point I thought all of me would shoot right up to the stars would continue. How long could such a feeling last?

After that, I wasn't sure where to take this. I could think about it tomorrow.

"Wake me to stand guard when it's your turn to sleep," I said with a yawn. Truly, it was all I could do to remain awake. His arms felt warm and secure around me, and I couldn't imagine anything better than snuggling against his bare chest. He smelled good, like the river we'd bathed in and a hint of the forest.

Who would've guessed I'd start falling in love with an orc? I'd be dishonest with myself if I didn't name it, though I'd keep that to myself. I wouldn't want to give Zickar hope that there could be something between us until I was sure of it myself.

Somewhere between wondering what it would feel like if he touched me in that hot spot between my legs and him resting his chin on the top of my head, I fell asleep . . .

I woke to him stroking my back.

"Time to take watch, mate," he said softly. "Or sleep more if you want. I can do all the watching."

"I'm awake." I smiled up at him. "I had the best dreams, though I don't remember exactly what they were." Oh, I remembered, but talking about it? I wasn't sure how to do such a thing.

In my dreams, I was with him. We walked in a meadow holding hands. And he kissed me again. I couldn't recall more than that, but it was amazing.

I'd never believed dreams could foretell the future, but my heart had flown high into the sky during that moment, as if there was no place and no one I'd rather be with than him.

"Do you need to change your position?" I asked.

At least his hard-on was gone. I'd heard it could be painful. Why would males wish to have one if it hurt?

"No, I'm fine," he said. "I'll sleep and you can keep watch."

I pulled the knife he'd given me from the sheath at my waist and gripped it tightly, easing back to the point where I could shift off his lap. I'd remain awake better if I wasn't nestled against him.

Before dawn, he woke on his own, stretching his arms overhead. He really was gorgeous, but his beauty didn't come solely from his surface. That was fleeting.

We all changed as we made our way through life. But Zickar was a gorgeous person inside where it counted.

"I'll hunt," he said. "I'd like you to remain here. Keep your knife close." He adjusted his long blades, strapping the lower parts of the sheathes to his thighs to hold them in place.

With that, he leaped off the tree. While my heart erupted into my throat, he grabbed onto the branch of another tree and swung to the next, soon disappearing from view.

I pivoted to lean against the tree and waited.

Within an hour, he returned with three reskits slung over his shoulder that he'd already cleaned. After helping me to the ground, we roasted the meat, ate about half, and packed the rest to eat later.

My clothing was dry, so I went behind a bush and dressed in my pants and shirt, carefully folding his tunic and placing it in his bag. We started walking.

"Could you tell me more about your clan?" I asked, not sure what to expect. In the village, we were told orcs were wild beasts roaming the forest, but how could that be true when they'd negotiated a treaty with such skill? No one knew how they lived, actually, though a few suggested they built crude huts and huddled inside them. Or lived in caves.

Women selected for the hunt shuddered at the thought of making such places their new home.

"We in the Matis Clan live both above and below ground," he said.

I tried to picture what he meant. "Why both ways?"

"From the time my people settled in the forest ages ago, some preferred the sunlight, while others sought sanctuary from shaydes and ashenclaws beneath the surface."

"Do you mean in caves? I've heard there are such places beneath the soil."

"We lived in caves at first." He held a branch to the side for me to pass him, and we continued following an overgrown trail up a hill and down the other side. "Then they located a vast cavern system below ground and moved there."

"It must be very dark underneath the dirt." My skin quivered at the thought of huddling below the surface, sitting on a stone floor, and worrying that each touch on my skin could be an insect.

"It is dark in some places, but we cultivate whisps."

"They need a breath of air to glow." We even used the insects for lights.

He lifted his pendant. "They also respond to our call."

"I saw you blow on your pendant to call Taen."

"And usually, he responds. We're able to make a broad range of sounds with our pendants for various reasons."

"Like calling to a friend?"

He nodded. "Or to tell others about danger. As for living underground, it's quite beautiful there. A clear river runs through the area where some of my clan lives, and there are falls and pools to swim in. We grow vast gardens there, irrigated by the river. It's cool in the summer, and it doesn't get as cold in the winter when it snows in the forest."

Maybe it wouldn't be so bad after all.

"You mentioned others live above ground?"

He waved his hand upward. "In the canopy itself. We've built platforms and discovered pendant tones can be used to guide the vines."

Since I'd never enjoyed heights, perhaps I should live beneath the ground. "Where do you live?"

"In the canopy, though once I return to my clan, I'll set up a home below the ground as well."

I frowned. "Why two homes?"

"Because I will soon take the role of caedos."

CHAPTER 12
ZICKAR

"You said caedos means leader," Alwen said. "Your friend was *caedos.*"

"As his younger brother and second, I'll be expected to step into that role when I return. We'll mourn Dakur." I growled, wishing I could go back and kill those men again for taking such a wonderful friend and caedos from us. "But after we mourn, we need a leader. I always thought..."

"What?"

"That his son would take the role when Dakur decided it was time. He'd recently talked of finding a mate, of perhaps going to the mate hunt, but he never got the chance." Anger tasted bitter on my tongue.

"I'm sorry. I wish I could've helped him, but they kept me tied from the moment they captured me."

"You said he never moved. He might've been dead already."

"Perhaps. It's not fair to die alone like that. I could've sat with him, stroked his forehead."

My mate would be the perfect partner for our clan's new caedos. "Thank you."

We walked the rest of the day, not stopping to do more than take care of our needs in the woods, drink from the river, and eat the rest of the roasted reskit.

Before dark, I started looking for another good tree, though we'd bathe first in the river. It didn't take long to locate one, and I hung my pouch on a low branch, and we walked to the river.

I loved how comfortable my mate was with me already, how we'd become friends. I'd need a good friend when I took over leadership of the clan.

The role of caedos could be lonely.

At the riverside, I turned away to strip, trying to ignore the rustle of her clothing. She tugged on my tunic, then crouched beside the river to wash out her things.

"I'll have clothing made for you once we reach our clan."

"That would be nice." She smiled up at me while I fumbled with the tie on my loincloth. "I've never had a lot. Mostly things given to us from others that my mother remade to fit me. With three siblings, we struggled to feed ourselves, let alone put clothing on our backs."

What would she think if I told her she'd soon live like a queen? That her family would be respected and appreciated living with our clan?

"You can have many dresses or pants if you prefer. As my mate, you'll also have someone to help you settle into the clan."

She frowned, her hands stilling on her shirt as she was draping it over a rock to dry. "You mean like a servant?"

"Somewhat."

"I don't need anything like that. I can cook our meals and keep our home tidy."

"Anyone's welcome to cook in their homes, though most eat in the community dining area."

"Then I can keep our home clean. I'd hate to put anyone out. I'm sure everyone's needed."

"We'll . . . discuss this again when we reach my clan." I would show her my home in the canopy, and she could help me select one below ground and furnish it how she pleased. She'd then see how well we lived when compared to humans.

Even Dakur had lived what many would consider a palatial lifestyle. He hadn't liked it and grumbled quite a bit about how lavish his home was. But it was expected of the caedos. When dignitaries from another clan visited, he couldn't entertain them in squalor. They expected the equivalent of a palace, and that's what he showed them, though he'd only used one room in that treetop home himself.

"Do you happen to have another tunic I can wear? Although I could wash this one in the morning before we leave, and it can dry as we walk."

"I don't have any others. I only brought it and a pair of pants in case I needed them. I planned to wear my loincloths most of the time."

"They look good on you." Her face darkened as she straightened, her gaze flitting away from mine. "I'm sorry. I shouldn't mention such a thing."

"That you find me attractive?" Frankly, it heartened me. I was beginning to worry we'd only remain friends. I wanted more. Her as my mate. Her lying in my bed each night, welcoming my touch. I could remain patient for as long as it took, but it was natural for me to wish for more.

Her head tilted, and her fingertips tightened on the hem of my tunic.

I turned away to give her privacy.

"Do you find me attractive?" she asked.

"Why else do I call you pretty maiden?"

"I thought you used the phrasing to taunt me."

"I use it because it's true."

She puffed out her breath. "I don't mind that you find me attractive. It doesn't scare me."

And I could work with that.

She tossed my tunic on the shore and splashed into the water. Once she called out, I finished removing my loincloth, washed it, and hung it to dry. I strode into the river, and the cool water felt amazing on my overheated skin.

I handed her the soap, and we bathed, keeping distance between us. Then she surprised me by swimming right up to me. Pink colored her cheeks, and her eyes remained on my chest.

"I, um . . . Can I ask you to do something for me?"

"Of course."

I expected her to ask me to help rinse her hair or to comb it for her like I'd done the night before. When she didn't speak, I nodded.

"Before we eat and climb a tree, would you be willing to kiss me again, to touch my breasts, this time without clothing between us?" she said in a rush.

Blood roared through my veins, stiffening my cock immediately.

"You don't have to do this if you don't want to," she said shyly. "I realize this is probably something you'd begrudgingly do, but I want to see how it feels. I need to find out if it's as nice tonight as it was last night."

My longing for my mate was going to kill me.

CHAPTER 13
ALWEN

"I love touching you," he said, his voice deep and husky. "It's never something begrudgingly done."

"I know you're tired. You probably want to dry off and dress, then go to our camp and eat. We still have to climb a tree, or you have to climb and haul me up with you. Then you won't get a solid night's sleep before you have to go hunting."

"I don't mind doing any of this."

I wasn't sure why my emotions were in such a turmoil. I felt drawn to him when I shouldn't. A male had done a horrible thing to me. Surely, I should avoid them all.

But I couldn't seem to drum up that feeling with Zickar. I enjoyed being with him, talking with him.

And I loved looking at his body. Even his big cock didn't scare me one bit. I actually wanted to touch it, stroke it, and if it came to that, I wanted to discover what it felt like inside me. I had a feeling the act wouldn't hurt like it had that one time, and I wasn't sure what to think about that either.

Not only that, but I also wanted to find out what his smaller cock would do.

"I'm glad you don't mind," I said. "But I feel like I'm placing yet another burden on you when I ask you to kiss me and touch my breasts."

His soft groan rang out, echoing across the water. "Alwen. You're incredibly inexperienced."

"And that's the problem. I've had one bad experience, and nothing else to compare it to." Irritation with myself churned through me, and I spun, determined to swim to the shore and not bring this up again.

He caught me from behind, his arms going around my waist. And when he tugged me back against his chest, his cock prodded stiffly between us.

Why wasn't I scared of his erection? I gnashed my teeth. How could I go from feeling terrified about sex to . . . all right, craving it. Somewhat.

"It's all right to feel conflicted about this," he said by my ear. "It's natural."

"How can it be? I should be terrified of all this. That man told me I made him want me, that it was my fault it happened." I was desperate for Zickar to understand. "But I didn't do anything like that. I barely knew he existed until the moment he cornered me and wouldn't let me go. I surely didn't make him drag me to his home and force himself on me."

"You didn't do anything wrong," he snarled. "He's to blame for it all."

I also loved how protective Zickar was of me.

I turned in his embrace, watching the emotions tumble across his face. Anger, determination, and a flash of kindness I sensed was directed toward me.

"I want to kiss you," he ground out. "I want to touch your breasts, suck on your nipples, do the same with your clit and push my fingers inside your tight little passage. I know you'll despise me for saying it, but I want my cock there too. The need to drive it into you is nearly sending me out of my mind. But I will never, and I repeat, *never*, do anything like that to you without your permission. No, without you telling me outright you want it. *You* have done nothing to drive me to this moment."

My breath caught—but again, not with fear. More with wonder and a warm feeling enveloping my heart.

"I'm sorry I said all that." This time, he turned away from me. "I've shared too much, wanted too much, when I have no right to say it. I don't want to put pressure on you."

"It's all right," I said, my voice shaky. "I'm glad you're being honest with me. That's what friends do."

"Alwen, I want so much more than friendship from you. My clan's pendant chose you as my mate. It would be dishonest of me not to tell you that I want it all. Your heart, your every moment, and your body. But I'm a patient male. I'll wait forever in the hope that one day, you trust me enough to let me touch you in every way possible. If not, that's all right too. We're mates, and I'm going to protect you and take care of you no matter what."

I suspected I'd soon want him as much as he did me—both emotionally and physically. I just needed time.

"Back to your request, because I want to focus only on that. Only on now. I'd decimate everything around us for the opportunity to kiss you and touch your breasts," he said, his voice cracking.

My chest hurt so much; I couldn't breathe. My air wasn't going to flow easily again until I'd made this male happy. Only then could I be happy with myself.

Should I tell him it was all right to touch me now? I wasn't experienced in things like this, though I was aware that some women enjoyed the sexual act. I hadn't quite believed it until I met Zickar, until he kissed me and touched me.

He tipped my chin up and his mouth came down hard on mine. I froze but only for a moment. This wasn't the other male, but the orc I was rapidly . . . Yes, I was beginning to love him. The feeling had crept up on me, jumped me actually, and dragged me down into its embrace. There was no place I'd rather be than with him.

I opened my mouth, gasping out a moan, and his tongue joined mine, thrusting within me fiercely. I could imagine his cock doing the same thing, and for the first time, the thought made my blood pound with excitement.

He softened his lips, his hand gently cupping the back of my neck.

And when he touched my right breast, when he rolled the nipple, fire shot through me, centering in my core. I pressed myself against him. When I wrapped my legs around him, his stiff cock slid between my legs. I rocked against him, and his cock rubbed against something there that made me feel amazing. Shock poured through me, and I bucked against him harder, my head tipping back and my mouth opening to release moans I couldn't believe came from me.

Something latched onto that area and vibrated. My harsh moan rang out, and I moved against him faster, overcome with sensations I'd never imagined in my life.

When I opened my eyes, he watched me, one hand supporting my back—urging my hips forward when I thrust against him. I'd never imagined how wonderful it could feel for someone to touch my nipples. How decadent. His pendant blazed again, and he ducked his head as if he was embarrassed by it, though I couldn't imagine why.

Did the fates of his clan play a role in our growing feelings?

"Take what you need, mate," he said softly. Leaning over me, he trailed his lips along my neck, sucking and gently biting the skin. All the while, his hand teased my breast.

And I pumped against him. Nothing could stop me now. Something big was building inside me, tightening and loosening. I sensed it would let go soon, and nothing would stop me from claiming it as my own.

His cock grew stiffer, and he jerked his hips forward to meet my thrusts. Whatever sucked on me down there increased the speed of its vibration. Each time he drove his shaft toward me, shock waves shot through my body. I felt hot and achy. I sensed I'd die if we didn't finish whatever we'd started.

When he tugged on my nipple and bit down on my neck, everything let loose inside me.

I fell apart, and Zickar was there with his arms spread wide to catch me.

CHAPTER 14
ZICKAR

Nothing could be more beautiful than my mate finding her pleasure with my body.

When she came, so did I, my cock shooting hot spurts into the water.

My pendant stopped flaming. It would blaze again intermittently until I came inside her, but for now, it was as satisfied as me.

Alwen's legs dropped down beside mine, and she pressed her forehead against my chest, holding my sides until her ragged breathing smoothed. I stroked her wet hair, her back, and murmured inane words I might not remember later but fit this moment.

I believe I even told her I loved her, though how could that be true?

"It'll be dark soon," she eventually said, still not looking up at me. "We should dry and dress and eat."

"We do need to be up in a tree before the sun sets."

We'd walk tomorrow and rest again tomorrow night, then reach Matis territory by midday the next. I couldn't wait to have others around to keep watch.

I hadn't told Alwen I suspected we were being followed. I'd scoured the area while hunting yesterday but found no real evidence. Yet I couldn't shake the feeling I'd be foolish to ignore.

The itching feeling on the back of my neck hadn't abated since we left the first meadow. Then, I thought I'd seen impressions near the clearing indicating someone else had been near our camp not long before, but I'd found nothing further when I scouted the area.

Tonight, after Alwen was secure in a tree, I'd go hunting for anyone spying on us. If I found no evidence of anyone near, I might be able to shrug off this feeling.

That wasn't the only thing plaguing me, however. There was a good chance things would change between Alwen and me when we reached my clan, and I wasn't sure there was anything I could do about it.

Madr, the prince of the orc kingdom, though the Matis Clan didn't observe things like that, had stopped with his mate while traveling to the orc city built by the sea. He and his mate had not yet solidified their bond, and as sometimes happened in my clan, the pendants of Matis males blazed, telling them she could also be their fated one.

To claim her once more, Madr had to compete with the other males in a series of tests. He'd won, and by the next morning, he'd fully claimed his mate. His pendant no longer blazed.

What would I do if the pendants of other males flared for Alwen? I'd compete with everything inside me, of course, but I could lose.

The only way to make sure she was my full mate forever was for us to be together completely, something I couldn't ask her to do. If she offers her body, it should be because she wanted me as much as I did her, not out of fear that someone else might say she was his.

I'd trust the fates to handle this; there was nothing else I could do.

We ate and took care of our final needs, plus stretched out our wet clothing on branches to dry then I located a good tree for the night. With my needed supplies hooked to my loincloth, I helped her climb, but when we reached a secure branch, I remained standing.

"I'm going to hunt." And look around to make my inner beast stop twitching. I nudged my chin toward her knife. "I won't be long."

Sitting with her back against the trunk and the blade lying on her lap, she frowned up at me. "Why not hunt first thing in the morning like you did before?"

Because I wouldn't be able to sleep until I was sure nothing was stalking us.

"I saw reskit tracks earlier," I said. "I'll set a few snares on the trail, hopefully snagging a few when they return to their dens." This was actually true.

Her posture loosened, and she yawned. "All right. I'll

stay here, of course." She shot me a smile. "It's not like I can go anywhere on my own."

I didn't like that she was trapped high in a tree, but she was safer here than on the ground.

With a nod her way, I leaped to the right and used a branch of a nearby tree to swing to the next, moving through the canopy. I'd drop to the ground eventually, but I didn't want to leave scouting tracks someone else might find on the forest floor.

When I'd made my way half a clik or so away from where I'd left Alwen, I swung lower, releasing and landing squarely on the ground. Remaining still, I listened, but I didn't hear anything but the howls of ashenclaws in the distance. They didn't sound as if they were coming this way, and they'd be spooked if they'd caught our scent.

Where was Taen? I'd tried to tell myself he'd been hit with the mating call himself, that he and another shayde were busy making tiny shaydes, but it didn't settle right inside me. I was missing something, but I couldn't figure it out.

Had something hurt him? I'd found no evidence of that when I followed his tracks leading away from where I'd killed the two men. He hadn't swung around to return to me, and his steady, wide pace suggested he'd loped away from the area in the opposite direction.

I was torn between wanting to follow his tracks and get Alwen to a secure location and had to put her first.

Studying the ground and the area around me, I

slowly made my way in a wide circle around where I'd left Alwen, easing through the woods almost silently and doing my best not to leave evidence behind.

I didn't find any tracks other than old ones from small creatures, ashenclaws, and shaydes, common enough. This comforted me.

Why did I still feel as if someone had been following us for days?

Unable to shake the feeling, I made my way closer to where we'd left our clothing to dry, pausing to set a few snares where I could check them in the morning without worrying about leaving Alwen for long.

I carefully made my way back to the tree, taking a zigzag route that I hoped would throw off whoever might be watching.

I paused at the base of the tree where I'd left Alwen and listened for a long while, still hearing nothing of concern. Turning, I leaped and grabbed onto a branch overhead. I quickly made my way up, eager to hold my mate through the night.

But when I reached the branch, Alwen was gone.

CHAPTER 15
ALWEN

The stone man had found me.

I'd told myself the last thing I'd do while Zickar was gone was sleep. Yet I dozed, rousing when the branch shifted beneath me.

My yelp was cut off by stone man's hand landing over my mouth. He grabbed onto the front of my tunic and hauled me up and held me with my face pressed against his chest so snugly, I couldn't cry out. It was all I could do to breathe.

I kicked and flailed, but his body was as impenetrable as the stone I'd named him for.

He jumped from this tree to the one next to it, then the one after that, the branches swaying and dipping from his weight, before plunging down to the ground. The world blurred past us as we fell. My belly erupted into my mouth, and I flinched as branches whipped his thick boulder arms and my back.

With a dull thud, he landed hard on the forest floor. He bolted through the woods with me clamped against his chest, needing only one thick hand to pin me in place. He didn't take a trail, just crashed through the underbrush, knocking down spindly trees with the stomps of his rocky feet and the thrust of his enormous thighs.

My heart fluttered, and I worried it would stop. Cold, dark fear grabbed hold of my spine and shook it. I hadn't been safe with the men who captured me, but they at least felt I had value. I wasn't sure why stone man had come for me. Had he been following us all this time? To think I'd bobbed in the water with Zickar, nestled peacefully in his arms at night, and sat near a fire eating meals, never suspecting this big male made of stone could be watching.

After he'd run quite a distance, he stopped. A dull thump in his chest was followed by another, each one sluggish and with an odd click at the end. With a twist, he flung me up onto his shoulder, the force of it knocking the wind from my lungs. While I struggled to breathe—to release even a whimper—he ran again, keeping a straight line as he plowed through the woods.

Didn't he realize he was leaving a trail Zickar could easily follow?

Knowing Zickar wouldn't stop until he'd found me gave me hope, but each of stone man's jarring steps took us farther from where Zickar left me.

He ran all night without appearing winded, never stopping to rest or lower me to the ground so I could try to escape. I kept struggling, trying to slip free, but he snarled, a grating, grinding sound two boulders might make when they rubbed together. His hand smacked down on the backs of my thighs hard enough to bruise, and another growl ripped from him. I suspected if I kept trying to get away, he'd hurt me worse than he already had.

Biting my lips, I braced my upper body with my palms on his back. I couldn't hold back my tears, though I hated that I gave in to them now. They drained me, and it wasn't long before I fell into a rough sleep haunted by shadows and enormous stone people who threw me to the ground and stomped all over me.

I woke at dawn and stared around with bleary eyes. I still lay on stone man's shoulder, but he'd left the forest and was rushing across a big, open, sandy plain with hills far in the distance.

Partway across the wasteland, he paused and looked around, but I'd already done it for him. No one was following; no one was near except a small herd of fleet-footed creatures with big curly horns. They took one look at stone man and whirled around, fleeing in the opposite direction.

Stone man lowered me to my feet. My legs crumpled, and I would've fallen if his meaty paw hadn't latched onto my arm and held me upright. My feet tingled as sensation returned, and my head spun.

He stomped one of his enormous feet and the ground vibrated beneath us.

Then it dropped away.
We plunged down.

CHAPTER 16
ZICKAR

It didn't take me long to find the trail. I saw no evidence of Alwen, but in my heart, I knew whatever had followed us for days had taken her.

At least they'd blazed a wide trail for me to follow. I quickly grabbed our things and stuffed them into my pack, securing it on my back. I rushed after them. I'd kill whoever took her, and then I'd shout out my fury and kill whoever it was again.

The trail made it clear who it must be. I'd only heard of the Flazant, people born from the boulders around us. Our elders shared tales of when they were allies, when we'd go to battle together. This was back when we fought off threats worse than them.

No one knows why we drifted apart. Perhaps those who would kill us had been eliminated. Or they'd fled so far away, both groups barely remembered the other existed.

How had one of the Flazant made its way to this area, and why had he taken Alwen?

Sadly, the stories I only vaguely remembered from childhood didn't give me any ideas about how I might defeat such a threat.

I continued moving long past where I needed rest. The Flazant was relentless, not stopping even once.

Finally, when dawn stabbed light across the horizon, I reached the edge of the forest and found myself floundering across a sandy wasteland. The sun beat down, a heavy weight on my shoulders, and my mouth grew parched. Other than pausing to sip from my flask, I didn't stop. And when I reached the end of the desert, though I knew larger wastelands like this existed beyond the woods where I now found myself, I didn't find a single track.

I spent the rest of the day moving slowly across the desert while studying the ground. While I found evidence of hooved creatures, I didn't locate the Flazant's heavy tracks.

He'd disappeared, and he'd taken Alwen with him.

CHAPTER 17
ALWEN

I cried out as we plunged down through a narrow, stony channel, continuing so fast and far, I got dizzy. My heart sunk farther. Even if I could get away from the stone man, there was no way I'd be able to get back to the surface, unless whatever device he was using to take us down would respond to my command.

We came to a jarring halt on a ledge surface with stairs cut into the rock. He dragged me down them and through a series of long passages, each with luminescent crystals coating the roof. They cast an eerie glow on both of us, making my skin appear blue, purple, and green to match.

Leaving the final channel, he swept me up and carried me into an enormous cavern with a roof at least five stories above. Stone spears plunged down, some with tips reaching almost halfway toward us. He strode around matching stone spears that appeared to have erupted from the rocky floor ages ago. Each of his steps reverberated, creating muted echoes—a constant reminder of just how deep below the surface we were.

Leaving the cavern, he walked through a short channel and into yet another big open space, this one with a cleared floor as if someone had removed the stone spears, leaving only those on the roof. A crystal-clear pool took up the center of the cavern, the banks covered with luminescent plants. Pale pink and yellow flowers bloomed on moss-covered rocks; their petals shimmering and fluttering as if alive under the dim glow emitted by the water. Beams of light reached out from the luminous plants, and when we passed a low hole in the wall, something dark and sinewy snapped out a limb and grabbed a handful of the flowers, dragging them back into the darkness.

The stone man entered a large cave along the far left wall. Striding to the back, he lifted me up onto a shelf that had to be twice my height above the ground. A fur covered the stone surface, and I took in two bowls, one holding water, the other holding the pink and yellow flowers.

Did he plan to keep me as a pet? Better that than a mate, though I didn't see a cock between his legs, and he wore no clothing.

Tremors rippled through the stone ground and walls around me, and I worried everything would collapse, that I'd be crushed beneath the weight of this world, and no one would ever find me.

Turning, the stone man left the cave—left me.

I peered over the edge, wondering if I dared risk injury by jumping from this nest. At this point, it didn't matter. I couldn't remain here, waiting to learn what the stone man planned to do to me.

After glancing toward the cave opening to make sure he wasn't returning, I scooted to the edge and sat, turning to lay on my belly and carefully lowering myself until I dangled from my fingertips.

I let loose and fell, landing hard on the rocky surface and falling back onto my butt. Sitting there a second, I assessed myself, but I appeared unharmed.

Rising with a rock in each hand, I crept along the outer wall to the opening and poked my head through, peering around the cavern. No stone man, but that didn't mean he wasn't lurking nearby.

Since I spied small holes low to the ground where the spindly limbed creatures might be hiding, I scampered fast past them, not stopping until I'd crossed half of the big open space. I crouched behind a boulder—after making sure there was no hole in the wall behind me— and caught my breath, listening and peering around. I still didn't see the stone man, but he wouldn't make all this effort to capture me and bring me here if he didn't plan to keep me.

When I felt I couldn't remain hidden any longer, I crept out from behind the rock and continued across the cavern, passing the pool and running up the slope leading to the channel between this big cave and the next.

It was dark inside the passage, but I clung to the wall and made my way to the end, peering out into the second cave, but still not finding the stone man. I bolted, racing across the big open space, and pressed my back against the wall beside the next tunnel.

Stomps rang out, and my heart froze. I crept backward, squeezing into a narrow channel in the stone wall, where I remained still, holding my breath.

The stone man walked out into the cavern followed by three other stone people—all much smaller than him.

They started across the big open area, but the tiniest one whose head might reach my chest paused and turned back. Its bright blue eyes glowed, seeming to pierce into the narrow gap where I'd wedged myself.

Its mouth dropped open, and it lifted its arm, pointing toward me. "Look, Dillu. It be a people."

I flung myself from the gap and raced into the tunnel with stomps and shouts echoing behind me.

I'd only made it halfway through the long passage when the stone man grabbed me. He hefted me off my feet and flung me over his shoulder.

With the smaller ones hopping around and chattering at his sides, he pivoted and took me back toward the cavern.

CHAPTER 18
ZICKAR

I wasn't giving up. I'd wander this desert forever, not stopping until I found Alwen. I'd never leave her behind.

But I couldn't find a trace of her anywhere, not that day or the next. I slept on the cold ground, remaining in the area, convinced I was missing something. If I kept trying, I was confident I'd find a trace of my mate.

The only change in the smooth sand I'd noted, what could be Flazant footsteps, stopped partway across the big open plain. I'd stomped around them, taking care not to disturb them, finding they ended abruptly. But unless the Flazant suddenly sprouted wings and took flight, traveling far beyond this area, I couldn't determine where he'd gone.

He'd taken Alwen, and I needed to find them. I knew very little about his species. Did they consume flesh? Would he hurt her like the man had in her past?

A shudder ripped through me at the thought of her helpless and at his mercy.

On the third morning, I left the forest and started across the plain again, determined to examine the area and find a clue I might've missed. The wind had blown the night before, but the tracks might still be there.

I stopped just beyond where the Flazant's footsteps ended and studied them. Seeing nothing new, I walked closer, though I didn't cross his path. I looked at his trajectory from all angles.

They came to a stop and then . . .

My clan used teegars to descend into the ground and for projection toward the canopy. The flat, smooth plants grew in circles. We carefully cultivated them, feeding them fillawate, a drink made from a very rare fruit that grows deep beneath the ground. We picked it in the fall and made the brew. The fruit itself contained properties that made the person drinking it feel happy. But when poured over the teegars, it gave them incredible energy, enough to reproduce and respond to our commands. In exchange for the brew they enjoyed, they transported us below ground or projected us toward the canopy.

Did a desert teegar exist? If so, it could've dropped down below the surface, taking the Flazant and Alwen.

I moved to the end of the Flazant's tracks and dropped to my knees, carefully brushing the sand around the footsteps.

In no time, I'd exposed a circular teegar. With a feral

grin, I stood upon it. I had no fillawate to offer. Would it respond to my pendant's call?

With one of my blades in my hand, I lifted my pendant and carefully blew across it. Nothing happened. My guts churning with frustration, I stomped my foot on the teegar.

It plunged downward, taking me along with it so quickly, I nearly toppled. Regaining my balance, I spread my feet to give myself better balance.

When the teegar reached the bottom of a long, narrow stone passage, it came to a shuddering halt. I stepped off it, and it shot back upward. I wasn't sure how to call it back, but I'd figure that out if I needed to use it again.

Turning, I studied the long tunnel stretching ahead of me. The stone floor gave nothing away, and I didn't hear anything to tell me where I might find Alwen. But I was convinced she was near. This was a start.

I took off at a jog down the passage, pausing intermittently to listen but still hearing nothing but the light trickle of water ahead.

Then a cry rang out. My heart froze.

There was no mistaking Alwen's shout. "No, no!"

Pulling my second blade, I bolted in that direction. It was time to rip a stone being apart.

CHAPTER 19
ALWEN

The stone man carried me back across the caverns quickly with the smaller ones clambering around us.

"Play wit, Dillu," one shouted. "Play!"

"Play, play," the other two chimed in. Their footsteps created rocky stomps, though not as heavy as his. Was he their father? If so, where was their mother, assuming the stone people had parents?

"Play," the first whined. Stone man just grunted.

He brought me to the cave again and placed me on my feet gentler than I'd expect.

The smaller ones crowded around, chattering.

Make it crawl.

Feed it.

And my least favorite when it came to stone people.

Jump on it.

"I'm not an it," I said.

Their eyes widened and their jaws dropped.

"It speaks," one said softly. "Speaks. Speaks!"

"You Ma?" the smallest one said. It stuffed its thumb into its mouth.

"I'm not your mother, if that's what you're asking." I pointed to the stone man. "Is he your father?"

They snickered, though the sound was more like the rubbing of rocks together than what I'd call laughter. But they *were* stone people.

"Then he's not your father?" I asked.

The tallest one shook its head. "Dillu."

Whatever a Dillu was. Oh, wait. "You mean that's his name? Dillu?"

The tall one nodded.

"Is he a friend or . . . your brother?"

The three nodded together. Brother then. Maybe.

I swore the stone man grinned. His mouth stretched wide, that is. He confirmed my assumption when he shook his head and chuckled.

"Play?" the littlest one said, its thumb popping out of its mouth and returning.

"I could, but you three are big and strong. You'll have to be careful with me." I had younger siblings. I was practically their second mother. "We could play a hide and find game if you want."

"Yes," the three cried, hopping around.

"No run?" the littlest said, frowning.

Could they blame me for trying to escape if I was given the chance? I might be willing to babysit for a day or so, but I wasn't going to stay here forever as their nanny.

"I won't run," I said. "But I can't remain here for long. My mate will be worried about me." Of that, I had complete confidence. Zickar would find me. He'd come barreling in with his weapons raised. Assuming he could follow the tracks left behind by the stone man.

The littlest one pouted.

"What are your names?" I asked.

"Trillie," the tallest said.

"Brillie," the middle one said.

I held up my hand, then pointed to the smallest. "Let me guess. You must be Crillie."

"Villideer," she said.

I couldn't tell if Villadeer was female, but to make things easier for me, I'd call them all females. We women needed to stick together.

"Villadeer's a lovely name," I said.

She gave me a shaky grin.

"Where are your parents?" I asked.

The three shrugged. Stone man dipped his head and sighed.

Hmm. "Are you three alone here?"

"Yes," they said at the same time. "Play?"

"Yes, I will. For now."

Dillu watched me for a long moment before shaking a finger at me, a gesture I took as a warning. Don't run again.

We'd see about that.

He backed out of the cave, leaving me with the children. If he was their brother, he probably needed a break.

Were their parents dead or had they left? I wasn't sure anyone would be able to give me an answer, so I let it go for now.

"To play hide and find," I said. "You three need to count to fifty. I'll run and hide, and you need to find me."

"What fifty?"

"Can you count?" Maybe numbers weren't a stone people thing.

All three shook their heads.

"Tell you what," I said. "I'll count to fifty, which is a slow series of numbers." To give them a demonstration, I used my fingers to count to ten. "While I'm counting, you three go hide somewhere. I'll look for you."

"This fun?" Villadeer appeared skeptical.

"Sure." I flicked my hands at them. "Go. Run and hide."

They looked at each other and shrugged before lumbering from the cave, the thuds of their rocky feet echoing in the small room.

I tried not to grin. I might be their captive, but I'd always enjoyed playing with children. I'd have some fun, and when Zickar got here, I'd leave.

"One. Two." I slowly counted, though I wasn't sure they'd understand. Did stone people not learn numbers or was the lack of a parent—or anyone else as far as I could see—holding them back?

When I reached fifty, I strode out of the cave.

The three of them stood in the next cave, leaning against the wall.

Villadeer giggled. I think that's what the rocky, grinding sound was.

"You were supposed to hide." I raced away from them and ducked behind a boulder, calling out. "You can't see me. This is hiding."

"Where go?" Villadeer shouted.

Stomps told me they were running this way. They rounded the boulder.

"There are." Trillie pointed.

"I was hiding." I straightened. "I'm going to go back into the cave and count again. You three need to hide like I did, and I'll find you."

They nodded in unison.

Not sure this was going to work, I went back inside the cave and called out the numbers to fifty again. This time when I left the cave, I didn't see them around.

But when I strode over to the boulder, I found them huddled behind it, snickering in their grinding way.

"Um, hmm," I said. "Maybe we should . . . have a snack, then. We can play hide and find or make up a different game after that."

"Eat, eat, eat," they chanted, following me back to the cave.

Spying Dillu standing by the pool, I waved his way. "Hey, they're hungry. Do you have any food?"

He nodded and waved to the cave, suggesting he wanted us to wait there, that he'd bring something to us.

I could deal with that. There didn't appear to be any cooking items unless I'd somehow missed their kitchen. I had a feeling they didn't have one.

We trooped back inside the cave, and I found four decent-sized rocks for us to sit on in a circle. We'd barely settled before Dillu stomped into the cave holding a flat rock with mounds of something tan on top. I was hungry, but maybe not hungry enough for whatever he'd brought. However, I'd always felt it was important to accept the nuances of other cultures, though I was rarely exposed to them. I'd try whatever he offered, and I could forage later if I was still hungry.

He settled within our circle and placed the flat rock in the center between us. The little ones dove in, scooping up the mounds and stuffing handfuls into their mouths. Dust and bits of rock rained down their fronts, but from their groans, they were enjoying the meal.

They were eating sand he must've collected near the lift.

Dillu scooped up and offered me the final mound, and I stared down at the grit in my hand.

This was going to be a very long day.

A FEW DAYS LATER, the girls could count to twenty—almost—and they'd figured out how to play hide and find. It took me quite a bit of time to find them the last time.

Since I didn't eat sand, I went fishing, though I didn't have any equipment. But the fish here didn't appear concerned about me. As I slipped through the waist-high water, they floated around me. It was easy enough to scoop them up and toss them onto the shore. The girls would grab them and race around with them held aloft, shouting.

Fire to cook the fish gave me quite a challenge, but I wasn't sure I should eat the fish or the tubers I dug on the bank raw. When I explained what I needed, Dillu helped me collect wood and brush from the caverns beyond this one where spindly trees grew. When I'd mounded them in a shallow depression I scraped from the dirt near the pond, he rubbed his stony hands together, generating sparks.

Soon, the wonderful smell of cooking fish and tubers filled the air.

The girls giggled as I ate, no doubt puzzled by why I didn't want to eat sand.

On the third day, we played in the flat area on one side of the pond. I'd stood skinny rocks up from the ground like spears, and we tossed smaller, round stones toward them, keeping score of who knocked the most down.

Tired after the game, we ate again.

I sat on the shore after that while the girls dozed beside me. I couldn't stop worrying about Zickar. Where was he?

I missed him more than I ever thought I would. It

was like someone had sliced into my heart, grabbed a chunk of it, and bolted. I'd only feel complete when it— and he—was back with me.

How had I fallen in love so easily and what was I going to do about it if and when I saw him?

I could only hope he'd find me soon, because it was clear Dillu wasn't going to let me go.

CHAPTER 20
ZICKAR

Following an odd, grinding sound, I traveled through stone passages and entered a big open cavern.

I'd barely started across it when something enormous leaped from above, landing hard on my back and driving me to my knees. I rolled, still keeping a grip on my blades, and came up to a crouch, facing the threat.

A Flazant male—his nubby horns on his head gave away his sex—charged me. He was twice my size and width, and he held a club. His feral gaze met mine, and he growled.

He lunged toward me, and I sidestepped, swiping my blade at him as he passed. The tip clanged but didn't penetrate his rocky hide. His club swung out, and I ducked just in time to hold onto my head. Rolling again, I came up beside him, stabbing out with my blade again. It did nothing; not even a scratch.

He grinned and grabbed me around the neck, lifting me off the ground.

I kicked and gouged with my blades, but he was too far away. His grin only widened.

"Dillu," Alwen called out, standing at the mouth of a tunnel on the opposite side of the cavern. "Put Zickar down. He's a friend."

Dillu?

My face grew hot, and I struggled to breathe while Dillu glared at me.

"Dillu!" Alwen stomped her foot.

Three Flazant children crowded around her.

"Play," one cried, rushing down the hillside and across the cavern, her footsteps making the ground shake.

"Play, play," the other two chanted, following.

Alwen ran with them, coming over to stand beside Dillu. "I said put him down. If you don't, I'm not going to babysit any longer."

I had no idea what was going on. Babysitting?

With a grumble, Dillu lowered me until my feet touched the ground, though he kept his hand clamped around my neck.

The world spun and if he didn't release me soon, I was going to pass out.

"Please, Dillu." Alwen laid her fingers on his arm, and I braced myself to find a way to protect her if he latched onto her throat too. "This is my mate. If you hurt him, I'm going to be very angry."

This was the first time she'd called me her mate. If the world wasn't losing focus, I'd tip my head back and roar out my joy. Instead, I feared I was going to die before I got to tell her how happy her words made me.

My pendant blazed, and despite worrying I was about to die, I was grateful she appeared unharmed.

"Release him, and we'll talk," Alwen said softly. "I promise not to leave until you agree."

The Flazant stomped his feet but released me.

I collapsed on the ground, clutching my throat. Air whistled when I sucked in one deep breath after another, but at least I could breathe.

Alwen dropped beside me, putting her arm around my back. "It's all right. Breathe easily. He won't do that again." She snarled up at the Flazant. "You won't, will you?"

The stony male hung his head and finally nodded.

"Play." The other three crowded around. "We play."

"What's going on?" I croaked.

"From what I can tell, though I've only been able to piece this together while I waited for you to come for me, the men who captured me somehow came across Dillu and his sisters. Seeing how strong and easygoing he was, they grabbed him. He could've easily broken free, naturally."

Dillu grunted and nodded.

"But they threatened his sisters. If he didn't help them, they'd kill the little girls. How could he let that happen?"

"Not . . . easygoing," I croaked, rubbing my aching neck.

"Well, it's a matter of perspective," she said. "I will admit he startled me when he grabbed me and ran, but he's been otherwise kind. He brought me here, and I've been playing with the girls, plus teaching them their numbers, while I waited for you to rescue me."

"You knew I would," I croaked.

"Of course." She flashed me a smile. "We're mates. You'd never abandon me." Sighing, she leaned against my side, and I put my arm around her, holding her close. I thought I'd lost her, that I'd never see her again. In the short time we were together, I'd come to love her. I couldn't imagine trying to go on without her. "I don't believe this is Dillu and his sister' original home. I think something horrible happened to their parents. Maybe they were traveling together or . . . I'm not sure what. But he's done the best he could to provide for them in this cavern."

"Why did he take you?"

"I believe he didn't know what to do with them. When he escaped the men, he circled back, watching us. Something must've told him I was female, and he's indicated he believes it's a female's role to raise children. He doesn't speak, but I've pieced that together by quizzing the girls and his grunts when I asked yes and no questions. But he's also made it clear he'll come after me if I try to run away."

"We're not remaining here forever while you to raise his sisters."

She frowned and studied the four who looked at us with what I suspected was hope in their eyes.

"Since we can't leave them," she finally said. "We'll have to take them with us."

CHAPTER 21
ALWEN

"Go wit where?" Trillie asked, her siblings staring at me with puzzled expressions.

"We're traveling to the Matis Clan," I said. I leaned close to Zickar and lowered my voice. "Would they be welcome there?"

"I would welcome them."

That wasn't exactly an answer, but he said he'd be the new caedos. Surely, he wouldn't allow his clan to kick my new friends out of their territory?

He pulled me aside.

Dillu hefted his club, but I waved him away. This was Zickar. He'd never hurt me.

"I don't know how my clan will respond if we bring them there," he said softly.

"You think they could reject them? You said you're the new caedos. Won't you be able to tell everyone they're welcome?"

"A caedos isn't a king who dictates to the others. I'd be caedos only because they agreed I was the right one to do the job. As for the Flazant family, we're careful about who we allow to enter our lands."

"I understand wanting to be careful, but I don't feel comfortable leaving them here."

"Their brother will take care of them."

"You heard what happened already," I said. "He's a gentle soul and easily taken advantage of. They all are."

"We could take them to their people."

"You said you're not sure where they are."

"It's true. I've only heard stories of the Flazant people. I guess, if we bring them with us to the Matis Clan, someone there might know how to communicate with their clan. Others might come get them."

"I don't have a problem with that, just leaving them here. Dillu's done an amazing job, but he needs help."

"You have a kind heart, mate," he said, tugging me into his arms. "I was terrified something horrible had happened to you."

"I'm safe." I pressed my cheek against his chest, and his steady heartbeat soothed me. "I missed you." I lowered my gaze. "Being with you. Talking with you. And when we swam in the river together."

He flashed me a tusk-filled grin. "We won't be alone again if they travel with us, though I'm sure we can find a way to sneak away to swim."

"I feel responsible for helping them even if that means we're no longer able to be alone."

"It's funny, but I also feel responsible for them. I can see the younger Flazants are sweet, innocent."

"They could be hurt much too easily."

"I'm not convinced anyone can hurt them. They're made of stone."

"Someone did. I think their parents are dead. If we leave them here, something worse could happen."

"Then we'll take them with us." He gave me a quick kiss.

I hugged him again and leaned back in his arms. "As for being alone, I'm sure we can find a little time here and there to ourselves."

He winked. "I look forward to it."

It was harder to talk the Flazants into traveling with us than I thought it would be. Surprisingly, it was the girls who put up the most resistance. They liked it here. The sand was particularly delicious. And they enjoyed the games we'd played together. It was only when I promised to show them new and even more exciting games as we traveled that they relented. They went to their cave and returned with bags strapped to their backs. Dillu traveled only with his club and a big bag full of sand.

"When I found the teegar, I found you," Zickar said, gesturing to the circular disc that had brought me down to this subterranean home.

"I've never seen anything like it before."

"Teegars are a plant. In my clan's territory, we foster

them, feeding them fillawate, a drink made from a fruit. It gives the teegars energy. We soak them in it periodically, and they, in turn, agree to transport us to the canopy or below ground."

"How do they eat?" I asked, crouching down to run my fingertip along the leathery surface. It twitched, and it was all I could do not to spring up and step backward.

"Like this," Brillie said, crowding over close to us. She spit at the teegar, and when it splattered on the smooth surface, it twitched and hummed, sucking down the liquid.

Dillu stepped onto the circle, and his sisters joined him, squishing together.

"We won't fit with you three," I said.

"Will." Trillie latched onto my arm and dragged me up against her rock-hard body while Brillie did the same with Zickar, giggling as she peered up at him through her spiky slate lashes.

His face darkened, and his lips twitched when he gazed my way.

The teegar shot upward so fast, my belly was left behind.

Dillu spread his arms wide above us, and when we reached the top, we burst through the surface and into bright sunshine.

Sand rained down on us, making me and Zickar cough. While we brushed it off, the others stepped away from the teegar. The girls scooped the sand off their bodies and ate it, crunching through the fine grains of rock.

Dillu shook like a chall, fluffy creatures we kept as pets. Sand scattered around him.

While Zickar peered in all directions, his hands on his weapons, Dillu bent near the teegar and spoke to it.

It shivered and started spinning before shooting downward. Sand trickled in to cover the area, and in a short time, it appeared as if there'd never been access to the subterranean world below us. Perhaps there was another entrance?

The girls waved as if the teegar could see them, before turning to Dillu and Zickar.

At Zickar's nod, we started walking, slogging through the sand that the girls kept scooping up and consuming. Dillu did the same, though he kept his attention on the area around us, seeking threats. Wise after what happened to him and his sisters.

The sun was setting by the time we reached the forest, and we decided to stop once we located the river, which Zickar said wasn't too far to our right. While I doubted shaydes or ashenclaws would bother my stone friends, there was no reason to take the risk. They were under our protection now, and we weren't going to let anyone or anything harm them.

Once we explained where we were going, Dillu forged the trail, knocking down spindly trees and stomping the underbrush until Zickar told him firmly to stop.

"The trees are our friends," he said. "We don't harm them." He showed Dillu how to move through the forest without stomping on everything, and we made quick progress.

The girls gazed around wide eyed. They must not have traveled in the woods before. Their people must live close to the desert. There wasn't much sand in the forest.

We found the river quickly, and I stooped down along the shore to cup some to drink.

The girls splashed into it, squealing.

"Oasis," Brillie cried out, falling backward into the water, creating an enormous splash that zipped up the shore.

The other two giggled and did the same, and soon, the water was churning. Dillu stood on the shore, grinning at his sisters' antics. It wasn't long before he leaped and splashed down in the water himself, sending a wave my way that was so high, it sloshed across my waist and nearly knocked me down.

Fish lay on the bank, and I gathered them up with Zickar.

"Look at that," I said. "They're contributing already. They gave us dinner."

His laugh snorted out. "They're fun."

"Thank you," I said. "I know you were hesitant to bring them with us."

"Only because of the ways of my clan. I could no more leave a friend behind than you could."

"They're pretty much family now. I feel a bit like an older sister."

"You have a good heart, mate. You'll make a fine caedos's partner."

We started cleaning the fish, washing away the entrails in the water.

"What will my role be in your clan?" I asked.

"An honored one. Many will turn to you for advice."

"I'm not sure I'm qualified to give anything like that."

"You'll learn," he said. "No one expects you to slip into the role immediately. Many of the prior caedos' mates worked with Tenkaril, our most revered elder. She raised me after my parents were killed by ashenclaws. Be aware, she'll want to *see* you."

"I'll be happy to meet with her. I want to learn all I can." I was beginning to look forward to standing by Zickar's side, to doing whatever I could to help his people—my people, now too.

"When I say *see*, I mean she'll want to touch your eyelids and look into your future."

I scoffed, but my humor fell when I realized he was serious. "No one can foretell the future, can they?"

"She has an uncanny way of knowing what might happen next."

"Can knowing what could happen bring about a change? You said *might*."

"Sometimes." He paused while stringing one of the four fish together. We'd have enough for tonight and in the morning. "She saw for me before I left."

"What did she see?" I washed my hands in the water, watching his face. The Flazant kids had stopped splashing and were floating downstream with the current. I couldn't believe that stones could float, but just because their exteriors felt like rocks didn't mean that was what their insides were made of.

"I'm not sure what she saw, but she told me one thing."

"What's that?"

"When you find them, it's vital you listen."

"Do you think they saw my new friends?"

He shrugged and watched as they played in the water. "I don't know, but it would surprise me if it didn't."

"Well, you listened to me," I said, leaning into his side. "They're here with us."

He nodded, and we turned and walked up the bank to start building a fire to cook our fish.

By the time night fell, our bellies were full, me and Zickar with fish and our friends with handfuls of sand.

"Will we have enough sand for them?" I asked, worried we'd reach his clan but be unable to feed them.

"Lots." Brillie opened the pack she'd carried, revealing more, as did Trillie and Villadeer.

It might seem like enough for a long journey, but they ate often.

"Enough," Trillie said, and I hoped she was right.

"Before we climb a tree, mate," Zickar said, holding

his hand toward me to pull me up from where I sat by the dying coals. "Would you like to swim in the river?"

My skin tingled at the suggestion in his voice.

We were going to swim, but I could tell he was ready for me to take my lessons in pleasure farther.

CHAPTER 22

ZICKAR

I felt like a lifetime had passed since I was alone with Alwen, and I was going to make the most of it.

We walked for a ways up shore from where we left the Flazant siblings, far enough where we could talk without being overheard.

We stopped on the shore and stared at the water reflecting the moon and the vast heaven full of stars overhead.

"It's beautiful here," Alwen said. "There's something so peaceful about it. I know the forest holds many dangers and that we need to be alert at all times, but look at it, would you? It's just lovely."

"You're lovely." I was watching her more than the view. She mesmerized me. I thought I'd lost her, and I wasn't going to risk doing so again. I'd hold on to her at all times if I could.

"Thank you." She gave me a shy smile. "Let's get undressed and wash so we can play in the water, shall we?"

My heart tripped over itself. Did she mean what I hoped for above everything else? My cock shouted it thought so and started rising, but I still sensed she might not be ready to complete our bond.

"There's nothing I'd like better," I said, my voice low and husky with emotion.

My pendant blazed, shining with the hope of my clan. It had chosen her for me, and I would thank the fates daily for gifting me with this woman.

With a soft smile, Alwen tugged my tunic up and over her head. "I'll wash it after."

We'd brought our bags, and she'd changed into her pants and shirt while my tunic dried.

I gaped as she slid the tunic up and over her head, revealing her gorgeous body.

"I didn't turn around yet," I said, trying not to drool.

"I don't mind. Your gaze feels like a caress, and all your caresses are good." With that, she strode into the water, stopping to look back at me while the water sloshed around her waist. "Are you going to stand on the shore all night, or are you going to join me?"

My cock stood at attention, poking the front of my loincloth.

Her gaze slid down my body with a light touch that set me ablaze.

I wrenched at my loincloth while she chuckled and dove into the water. By the time she'd surfaced, I was fording the river to reach her, my cock a stiff pole and my heart on fire.

I caught up with her and playfully teased my fingers down her spine, grateful to see only joy in her eyes. Not a touch of fear.

I helped her wash, my fingers stroking her breasts and her delectable ass.

When I slid my hand between her legs, she stilled and looked up at me with a mix of curiosity and excitement.

"I know what happens there, but I've learned that my experience isn't anything near what I'll find with you, mate," she said.

"I want to touch you. Just that," my voice choked off with emotion. "We don't have to take things further."

"I think we will go farther, but is it all right to wait?"

"I'll wait forever for you, Alwen."

She flashed me a smile. "I don't think it'll take me forever to get where I need to be. Maybe just a little bit longer."

My hand had drifted from between her legs and now rested on her lower back.

She took it and moved it back. "Touch me. Show me what I discovered with you already. No, show me how it will be when you're my lover."

My groan ripped out, and my cock slammed against

my abs. "Spread your legs around me, mate." It was all I could do to think, let alone speak. She was giving me the most incredible gift: her trust.

I'd never do anything to betray her.

CHAPTER 23
ALWEN

I didn't feel even a touch of fear. I knew whatever Zickar did with my body would feel wonderful because he was touching me with love.

Maybe not the love of legends, but a warmth within his heart he felt only for me.

He hadn't spoken the words, but I'd caught that light in his eyes. It was mirrored in my heart.

I spread my legs around him, pressing against his big cock that also didn't frighten me, though I did wonder how something so long and thick was going to fit inside me.

My Zickar would find a way, and I knew it wouldn't give me pain.

I held onto his sides, and he let the water slowly carry us downriver.

His fingers traced up and down my back before one hand glided around to stroke my breast. When he rolled the nipple, I tipped my head back and let the wonderful feeling consume me.

While he brought my nipple to a hard, needy peak, his other hand gently slid across my belly to that place where no *real* male had ever traveled. Only a real male would give more than take, and that male was Zickar.

His fingers stroked through my folds, and damn but it felt good. Between sparks shooting from my nipple to that very area, plus the soft words he murmured in my ear, I was falling apart at the seams. Once I unraveled, I'd be all his.

Then he touched a part of my body no one else ever had. Heat jolted through me, and I looked up at him in awe.

"Does this feel good?" he asked as he rubbed.

Lost in the heady sensation, I could only nod.

And when he slid a finger inside me, I started unraveling a bit more. With each thrust of his finger, he ran his thumb across that spot that made fire lick across my soul. I clung to his arms and bucked against him, completely lost in my mate and what he was doing to my body.

When he added another finger, I relished the stretch, knowing it would feel like this when it was his cock inside me, not his fingers.

I rode his hand while he continued to tell me how pretty I was. How much he admired me. How brave I was to give him this chance to show me that loving like this could be special.

His fingers went faster, and I moaned and rocked against him, my belly hitting his cock while he drove his fingers up until they grounded deep within me.

And when I started spiraling, giving into the feeling only Zickar could give me, I locked my gaze on his, and let him see my very soul.

CHAPTER 24
ZICKAR

I lay on my back with Alwen draped across my chest, holding her as we floated downriver. We passed our clothing, and I used loose kicks to hold us in place.

"Is it always like that?" she asked softly.

"I hope so."

Her low laugh rang out. "You mean you can't make promises?"

She was only teasing, and I loved that she could do so about something like this. It showed me she was learning how to put her past behind her and walk with me into a future with infinite potential.

"I can promise to do my best to make sure you enjoy every moment you're with me," I said.

"Zickar," she sighed. "You're making me . . ."

"What?"

"Actually, you're not making anything happen. *I'm*

falling in love with you because you're kind and wonderful, and I can't seem to stay away."

My heart expanded against my ribcage, and it ached in a good way. I tightened my arms around her. "Mate," I growled.

"I was going to run away as soon as I could, but I don't want to run any longer. I'm yours, Zickar. Committed fully to you."

I turned her in my arms and dropped my legs so I could kiss her. She tasted like sunshine, the warmth of a fire on a cold winter's day, and a future full of love.

"Mate," I said again as I lifted my head. "I want to love you completely, but I will never push for this. What we have is enough for always. This I swear."

"I want to try, Zickar." Her gaze met mine, and the trust there made my heart soar all the way to the sky. "I'm ready. I know you won't hurt me."

"Our first time should be special," I vowed. "But I have nothing to offer but me. Not here." Should I suggest we wait until we reached my clan—*our* clan?

"All we need is you and me, right?" she said with a heady smile.

Like the orcs who'd come before me, those who may not have had fine homes or much to offer, I would give her everything inside me, all of who I was in this amazing world.

We swam to shore and stepped out, quickly drying.

"We're not doing anything back at the camp with our

friends," I said with a soft laugh. "And not in a tree, either."

"We should try this sort of thing in a tree some-time," she said, her grin matching mine. "I was very tempted by all you have to offer already. It could be fun."

Only a few shadows lurked in her eyes. She must be remembering her first experience. I couldn't wipe that away, not completely, but I could give her something wonderful to replace it. Hopefully, that would be enough.

Hopefully, *I* would be enough.

With shaking hands, I gathered our things, and we walked into the woods completely naked as if we were explorers of a new world who'd arrived here with nothing. In some ways, that was how it felt.

What Alwen and I would do was brand new for both of us.

I had to make this perfect.

I peered around, stopping to listen to make sure nothing was stalking us. A shayde chittered far in the distance. Could that be Taen? I prayed he'd return to us soon. I hated returning to my clan without him.

It was even worse to return without Dakur, however.

I had to push that from my mind. How could I give my mate everything if I wallowed in the sorrow that was so eager to grab onto me and drag me down?

Soon we'd reach my clan. Soon I would grieve with my people. And my mate would stand by my side.

My pendant blazed, lighting our way, as if the fates knew what we were about to do and approved.

When we came across a small open area, the ground covered in soft moss, it was as if the fates had seen my dilemma and given me a solution.

I spread the drying cloth on the ground, grateful the air was warm.

I tugged Alwen close and just held her. The touch of her skin on mine reminded me of how fragile yet strong she was, how she appeared as if she'd easily break. But the world had forged her anew, and she'd emerged from the tragedy of her past with an inner core that was strong enough to handle any challenge.

Tilting her head, I gazed into her eyes, marveling again at how lovely she was and how grateful I was that she was a part of my life.

When she smiled, I kissed her, softly at first but deepening my touch as fire blazed through me. I'd kept it unleashed inside me, and while I loosened the bindings, I wouldn't let it completely free. Each step I took toward the ultimate ending would be taken with infinite care and kindness.

No one would break this woman again. Not as long as I had fire in my bones and this fierce need to protect her in my heart.

We dropped to the ground, entwined. As we continued to kiss, I stroked her sides, her thighs, finding her breast and gently cupping it. I lay beside her with her on her back, and she arched her spine when I rolled her nipple. It peaked for me, a hard bud I couldn't wait to claim with my mouth.

I trailed kisses along her jaw and neck, nibbling on her flesh. Her moan ripped out, and she thrust her hips up. She was so responsive, so perfect. I'd treasure the gift she was giving me always.

Kissing down her chest, I stopped at her nipple, sucking it into my mouth and stroking my tongue across it. I teased the other, tugging and rolling, while she sighed with pleasure and caressed my shoulders.

"Zickar," she said. "I need something. Please."

I lifted my head. "I'll give you everything. This I swear." I kissed across her belly and spread her legs.

She parted them willingly.

Then I stroked through her folds. I crawled between her thighs and took her clit into my mouth.

CHAPTER 25
ALWEN

I was fairly innocent when it came to sexual pleasure, but I'd heard a few women speak about what went on in the bedroom with the people they loved.

Joy could be found there, and I was greedy enough to want to grab onto such a thing and make it my own. I knew Zickar could help me find that perfect moment.

While he licked me, his fingers teasing through my wetness, I moaned and bucked up against him. Everything was tightening and loosening inside me, and each time I tightened, I sensed I'd soon fall apart.

"Zickar," I sighed. I adored saying his name, touching him, and having him stroke me.

But I needed more. I needed what the other women had hinted at. I sensed when I found it with my mate, it would seal over the wound still seeping inside me. I'd bear the scars for a lifetime, but they'd fade as they should.

He and I would *make* them fade, because I wasn't willing to face a future without claiming him fully. He was mine, and I needed him in every way possible.

When he dipped a finger inside me, I bit back my cry of pleasure. I wanted to shriek and share how wonderful I felt, but we didn't need company during a moment like this.

"You're so wet, mate, but I'm going to make you wetter," he growled against my skin. The movement of his mouth drove me higher. I was soaring to the sky and there couldn't be a better feeling than that.

He added another finger, and the stretch of it made me freeze, though only for a moment. Knowing this was Zickar, that he was doing this with love in his heart, made my bones melt once more. I was soon caught up in the heady sensations, riding them while nudging aside every thought but him, rather than letting even a bit of fear take their place.

A feral feeling took over me, and I moaned and shifted my hips up to meet the thrust of his fingers. His tongue played with the bead at the top, the fountain of all the wonderful sensations he generated.

When I felt like I couldn't go much higher, he pulled out his fingers and licked them, staring down at me.

His cock was enormous, thick and long. It thrust up against his abdomen, pressing against that second cock that I suspected had given me pleasure already.

His body didn't frighten me. He didn't scare me. This

was Zickar, and the feelings he generated inside me came from the emotions we shared.

We were mates, and I couldn't wait to claim him.

"I could take you like this." He climbed over me, bracing his weight off my body. "Or like this." He rolled me to the side and eased himself behind me. "Or with you on your knees or . . ." A smile quirked one side of his mouth up. "Or you could ride *me*."

"Soon. I want to try it all. For now, lay on top of me. Show me your weight. Your love."

How had I gone from fearing this to feeling so greedy I wanted to grab onto his cock and shove it inside me?

His low laugh rang out. "I'm happy to oblige, mate, but for now? I don't believe we should remain away from the Flazants for long. We wouldn't want them to come looking for us."

"Just give me your cock now." I never thought I'd say such a thing, but my body ached, and I knew only Zickar could give me the satisfaction I sought.

"Mate. You humble me. I just don't want to hurt or frighten you."

"You can't, Zickar. This is you, not him. It will always be you. That's the difference. There's trust between us, a feeling that cannot be broken. Now take me, mate, because I have need of your body."

He growled but his grin shone through. "Tell me to stop at any time, and I will. I'm not what matters here, just you."

"Oh, I think you matter. Now show me how good it can be. Wipe away the past and replace it with memories of you."

I crawled down her body again and sucked on her clit, not stopping until she was clinging to my horns and thrashing her head on the drying cloth. Only when she was so saturated from my touch did I rise above her again. I placed the head of my cock at her opening, and she hitched her heels on my hips.

With my eyes locked on hers, I slid partway inside her. Damn, she was tight, wet, and wonderful. I was going to come from this start alone.

When she didn't freeze, and her gaze never wavered, I pushed forward some more.

She gulped and swallowed but gave me a smile that made my insides melt. "You're taking too much time with this, mate. I thought there was more thrusting involved."

Exquisite joy poured through me. I wasn't sure I could bear much more. I would happily have a relationship without sex, but knowing she wanted me as much as I did her made me feel complete. Almost, that is.

While my pendant blazed, I pulled back and pushed deeper within her, seating my cock in her tight sheath.

"Ahh," she sighed. "Now there's the difference."

I frowned. "Difference?"

Her hand tightened on my arms. "When you love someone, this is wonderful. There's no pain when love pushes it away."

"Mate." She humbled me, stunned me. And I adored everything about her.

My spur sought her clit and latched on, humming.

"Ah," she cried, jerking her hips up toward me. "That . . ."

"It's yours, mate. *I'm* yours."

While my pendant continued to blaze, I started moving inside her, slowly at first, gauging how her body responded, then faster at her urging. All the while, my spur vibrated against her clit.

Her gaze remained locked on mine, and there wasn't anyone more beautiful than Alwen giving into her pleasure.

"Zickar," she cried out softly, lifting her hips up to meet me. "You're mine. Always. Never forget that."

"How can I when I'm yours and you're mine as well?"

"Take me. Claim me. Make me yours for a lifetime."

I thought I couldn't love her more, but a heady feeling spread through me, searing through my veins and across my skin.

And when she fell apart, crying out her joy, I followed.

Breathing hard, I collapsed on top of her, though I held as much of my weight off her as I could. I rolled, taking her with me, and she lay across my chest.

She lifted her head and smiled at me sweetly. It made my heart ache.

"Love you, mate," she said. "Thank you for showing me how wonderful this can be."

I stroked her back. "Love you too, Alwen. Always."

My pendant's inner fire winked out.

CHAPTER 27
ALWEN

We washed quickly in the river, dressed, and returned to our friends, finding the girls sleeping and Dillu striding around the clearing, his club poised to smack whoever might come near. When he saw us, he strode over and looked at us both, nodding.

"So it should be," he said, and for one moment, I nearly cringed. He came up with something like this for the first time he spoke to me?

I didn't like that he knew what we'd been doing, but I shrugged it off. There was nothing wrong with us being together. It was natural.

As he'd said, it was how it should be.

"I'll stand watch," Zickar said.

Dillu nodded and joined his sisters, lying curled partway around them.

Zickar stroked my face and smoothed my damp hair. "Sleep, mate."

"Here?"

"For now. I'll wake Dillu partway through the night to take over."

"I can do my share."

"Let me do this for you. For us."

"You'll be tired tomorrow."

"No more than the rest of us, I don't think. No one sleeps well on the ground. Or in a tree, for that matter."

"We'll reach your clan soon, right?"

"Late tomorrow, if we're lucky, or early the next morning. We could push into the night if we're close."

"I'm excited to see where we'll live."

He tugged me into his arms. "Things will change a bit when we're there. I need to take my brother's place, one I never wanted for my own. But we'll find time to be together."

"I'll help all I can."

"We'll need your strength. We'll mourn Dakur's loss, but then, as always when we lose a caedos, we must do what's best for the clan."

He took my hand and led me over to the fire, urging me to lie down. I didn't think I'd sleep, but everything caught up to me and carried me away. I woke to Zickar dropping down behind me onto the ground. His arm went around me, and it warmed me through to be with him like this.

We were two halves that somehow made more than one when we joined together.

After eating breakfast the next morning, we walked.

The forest grew thicker, but Zickar was able to see a trail I'd miss even if I walked upon it.

We stopped briefly to eat lunch, then kept going. And with Dillu at the back and Zickar leading the way, we continued into the night with moonlight filtering down through the canopy above to guide our way.

At one point, Zickar stopped and lifted his hand. He looked back at us over his shoulder. "We've reached Matis Clan territory. In a short time—"

Orc warriors wearing loincloths like his and bristling with weapons dropped down from above and melted from the woods on all sides, surrounding us. When they saw Zickar, they sheathed their weapons and cried out with happiness.

He walked from one to the next, bracing each on their forearms, speaking softly. After, he joined me, the girls, and Dillu.

"We'll take to the canopy now," he said.

Dillu frowned and looked up. "Flazant remain on the ground."

"Our vine bridges will hold your weight."

The other males nodded, studying my Flazant friends.

"You climbed a tree when you grabbed me," I said.

"Prefer ground," Dillu growled. I suspected he wasn't going to change his mind.

"The ground it is. We'll make sure you're protected and have shelter." Zickar lifted his hand to one of the males, who nodded, indicating he'd take care of this.

"Where's Taen?" one of the other males asked, and Zickar explained how the shayde had hunted with him but had not returned.

They exchanged heavy glances but said nothing else about the shayde.

"Has Loobek returned?" Zickar asked.

Loobek was the other orc who'd ridden a shayde to look for Dakur. Zickar mentioned that they'd split up to cover more territory.

"Yes," one of the Matis males said. "He was unsuccessful."

"But the shayde came back with him?"

The male nodded.

"All right," Zickar said. "I must speak to Tenkaril before I share anything further." He nodded to Dillu and his sisters. "We also use teegars to ascend into the canopy. Are you sure you won't reconsider?"

"We live on the ground or below," Trillie insisted. The others clustered with her, wearing matching frowns.

"The orc who left will return and take you to a safe place where you can eat and rest," Zickar said. He turned to the other males from his clan. "My mate and I will walk the rest of the way with our friends."

The other males tapped their foreheads with two fingers and leaped as one, grabbing onto branches and swinging up to stand on them. They were quickly absorbed into the canopy and other than the vague rustle of leaves, I wouldn't know they were there. I watched as they moved deeper into the forest.

"It won't take long to reach our destination," Zickar said, holding out his hand.

I took it, and we walked with our friends. A while later, we came to a clearing, where Zickar stopped.

"We wait," he said.

"For what?" Brillie asked, looking around with a touch of fear in her eyes.

"Our most revered elder will arrive soon."

Her fear faded. "All right."

The young Flazants dropped to the ground and opened their sacks to eat.

"Tenkaril comes," Zickar told me. "As I said, she may ask to see. Don't be afraid. It doesn't hurt."

I nodded, peering around. Above, the canopy swayed, and subtle whispers reached me. The feeling of being watched sunk into my bones and shook me. I wasn't afraid, however, not with many of Zickar's warriors around. But I still wasn't quite sure what to expect. I'd chosen a future at Zickar's side, but what would that mean for my life in general?

An elderly orc woman strode from the forest on our right, her hand resting on the forearm of a big burly orc. She walked right up to us and stopped in front of Zickar.

"Welcome," she said, her milky eyes sliding from him to me and our Flazant friends. "I see you listened."

"I always listen to you, Tenkaril," Zickar said, leaning over to kiss her weathered cheek.

Tenkaril tilted her head and appeared to listen herself. "Where's Taen? I don't hear him nearby."

Zickar explained again that the shayde had taken off and not returned.

She frowned. "All right." Her blind gaze traveled over the Flazants again. "We'll notify their people they're here. What are your names, my new friends?"

"The eldest sister is Trillie," Zickar said. "The youngest Villadeer, and the middle child is called Brillie. Their older brother and admirable protector is Dillu."

"We'll ensure you're quite comfortable," she said, giving them a tuskless smile.

Dillu sighed as if the heavy weight he'd been carrying melted off his shoulders. His eyes glistened, and I gave him a hug, something that wasn't easy since he was so much larger than me.

"I have much to tell you," Zickar said. "It can wait, but not for long."

"The fates have chosen wisely, my son," Tenkaril said, her smile lifting when she looked my way. "Welcome, daughter."

Zickar held out his hand and tugged me to his side. "This is Alwen. The fates chose her for me."

"And your pendant no longer blazes. Are there orclings in your future, my son?"

"If the fates allow," he said, shooting me a grin. It faded fast, however.

"And Dakur?" she asked softly. Her body tightened. Zickar said she could foretell the future. Did she already know?

"He's dead," Zickar said. "I'm sorry. Know that I found revenge for his murder."

Tenkaril fell to her knees. Tipping her head back, she wailed.

Hearing the woman who'd raised me cry out with pain was like taking a spear through my heart. I dropped to the ground and tugged her into my arms, holding her while she cried.

"Why?" she asked, over and over. "Why didn't I see this?"

The damn fates. Why hadn't they told us? Then we could've prevented it from happening.

Her sobs slowed to sniffs. Alwen stood beside us, her hand on my shoulder, her eyes filled with sorrow. Tears trickled down her cheeks. My mate mourned with us, and nothing touched me more than this.

I helped Tenkaril to her feet and her assistant rushed forward to take her arm. But when he would've led my adopted mother back to her home, Tenkaril frowned, her gaze going to Alwen.

"You, I must read," she said in a trembling voice. "You were there."

"I was." Alwen's gaze shot to me, but she nodded. "You're welcome to do whatever you wish."

She held still while Tenkaril advanced toward her. "First, I welcome you again, daughter. I'm sorry you've arrived at a time filled with sorrow. My son . . . My beautiful son, Dakur . . ." She pinched her eyes shut before opening them again. "You saw what happened to my Dakur?"

Alwen explained.

"I must see as you did. You'll permit this?" my mother asked. "Know that sometimes, the fates hand me visions I wouldn't wish on my worst enemy. I may see what you did, or not. I may see what will happen tomorrow. The fates don't always let me see what I should."

Alwen swallowed hard. "Please . . . If you see something horrible about me or Zickar, don't tell me."

"Sometimes, knowing can change your fate." Tenkaril huffed. "You wouldn't want the tool you may need to make all the difference?"

"You're right." Alwen's spine stiffened. "Tell me all. Don't hold anything back."

"Only what I must."

This was how she always saw. If something couldn't be changed, she often held it back. Why would someone wish to know that their child was going to die soon if they couldn't stop it from happening? But often, a path hadn't been well cut through the forest yet. A slash in another direction could completely change a person's course.

"Your mate is smart." Tenkaril sent me a sad smile. "I'm glad you found her and brought her to us." She cupped Alwen's cheeks and stroked them with her thumbs. "Pretty. She'll give you strong orclings."

"That is up to the fates as well." My heart soared, however. I couldn't imagine how amazing it would be to hold my own child, to raise him or her well, to ensure that they became a good person.

"Indeed, it is," she said with a choke in her voice. "And they are much too fickle." While Alwen remained still, Tenkaril closed her eyes and ran her thumbs across Alwen's eyelids. Her gasp rang out, and my heart clenched tight. Had she seen something horrible for my mate?

Her hands flung up into the air, and she stepped backward quickly, bumping into her assistant who reached out and caught Tenkaril's arm, steadying her.

"Ah, so that is how it must be," Tenkaril said softly, her head tilted down as if she stared at the ground. But she'd been blind since she was sixteen, though our healers could never determine the cause. Only then had the fates given her this sometimes wonderful and sometimes horrifying gift.

"What have you seen?" Alwen asked, stretching out her hand to take mine. I squeezed it to show her I was here for her always.

Tenkaril looked up at me with her milky eyes that saw nothing and everything.

"You'll take your brother's place as you should," she said. "We have much to discuss, but it can wait until the morning."

"What did you see?" Alwen asked, her voice shaking.

"I saw nothing about you or Zickar, my sweet daughter. Rest comfortably tonight." She waved to the four Flazants who'd remained silent through all this. "Come with me. I'll see that you're settled and send someone to notify your people that you are safe. They'll come for you, and it's good that they will. We need to repair the relationship we allowed to fade. If we're going to survive what we will soon face, we'll need all the friends we can gather."

"What have you seen?" I asked, determined to take on whatever this challenge might be to protect my mate and my clan.

"As caedos, you will soon know, but that will wait for the morning." She waved to Pulost and Finsteg, two males about my age. "My remaining son will need guards."

"A caedos has never had guards before," I said with a frown.

"And a caedos has never been stolen from the clan and killed before either, so a guard you will have."

I sucked in a breath and released it, unwilling to argue with her about this now. We could speak later. "All right."

Turning away, Tenkaril clutched her assistant's arm, the four Flazants watching her solemnly. As she moved across the meadow, they followed, and her sobs shook her shoulders once more. "Dakur. My poor Dakur. What will happen now?"

One after another, my clansmales gripped my upper arms and touched their foreheads to mine, swearing fealty to me as caedos. If we had no previously established line of command, those interested in leading would step forward and declare their interest in the position. If there was more than one good choice, they'd compete in challenges to prove who was most fit to lead.

As Tenkaril entered the woods, most of the males followed. Finsteg and Pulost remained behind. They dipped their heads my way and grunted, their weapons drawn and their intent gazes taking in the forest around us.

I could protect myself, but a caedos wasn't easily chosen, and everything must be done to protect him or her from harm. Because my mother was so upset, and there was wisdom in what she asked, I'd allow this for now.

"What do you think she saw?" Alwen whispered, still holding my hand.

"I'm not sure." I tightened my spine. "I only know one thing. We'll mourn tonight and, in the morning, I must take over the leadership of my clan." This wasn't a role I'd ever thought I'd step into, but I'll do all I could to ensure that whatever I did from now on, I would make Dakur proud.

We started down the path Tenkaril had taken, heading toward the central area of my clan. Pulost and Finsteg walked behind us, one close by and the other dropping back to scout the forest for threats.

"What can I do to make this easier on your clan?" Alwen asked.

There was my generous mate, thinking first of me and my clan, not herself.

"Just be here for us."

"Of course."

"I'll bring you to our home. It's high in the trees, and I know you don't enjoy heights."

She gave me a tender smile. "They're bearable when I'm with you."

"We'll see what you think over the next few days. If you're still frightened, we can claim our home below the ground immediately."

"Like the one where the Flazants lived?"

"Very similar, though I promise, we have furniture and won't eat sand." It felt good to inject a bit of humor into such a sad situation. "I'm sorry we're beginning our new life together with so much sorrow. I wish Dakur was here. I was his second, and I'll do all I can to be a good caedos, but no one will ever replace him."

"I'm sorry." Her eyes glistened with tears once more. If only I could make all of this right. Sadly, that wasn't going to happen. But at least I had her with me.

I stepped onto a teegar, tugging Alwen onto the circular plant with me. One of my guards joined us while the other waited nearby. He'd follow once he was sure I was secure in the canopy above.

"This is much like the teegar in the desert except this one doesn't carry us completely to our destination," I said.

She frowned, looking up at me. "How does it get us there, then?"

I wrapped my arm around her, holding her close. "It projects us."

She gulped and pinched her eyes shut as I blew lightly across my pendant.

The teegar soared upward and tossed us toward the first wooden platform.

CHAPTER 29
ALWEN

I bit back my yelp as the teegar disappeared from beneath us and we continued flying.

"I'm not a bird," I shouted. "I'm not a bird!"

We landed squarely on a broad wooden platform. Thankfully, Zickar didn't release me from his arms.

"Are you all right?" he asked, and I nodded. "At first, it'll help to focus solely on where you're walking or exactly where you've placed your feet," he said as the second orc joined us. The first stood nearby, facing away from us with a weapon in his hand, scanning the area as if he expected threats.

Not a pleasant thought. Vertigo kept grabbing onto me and tipping me sideways. It was enough to worry about falling. I couldn't imagine what I'd do if I had to fight off an attacking beast.

"Are there shaydes in the canopy?" I asked in a voice shakier than I liked. Here Zickar was being brave and facing the future he'd never planned for, while I quaked like a child beside him.

I tightened my spine and decided I was going to make this work. This was my new home. *He* was my home. My silly fear of heights wasn't going to hold me back.

"Shaydes don't climb trees. None have so far, that is," he said. "Up here, there aren't many threats. A bird might swoop in and steal your meal, and a few creatures have been known to bite, but most are more afraid of us than we are of them." He puffed his chest. "I'm going to protect you from everything. Have no fear."

So easy to say.

No, I was going to trust what he said. I shook myself inside, telling myself to wake up and join the world around me. There was wonder and beauty here, and I'd use that to balance any lingering fear.

"We'll go to our home first," Zickar told the males with us. He nodded to me. "This is my mate, Alwen. Protect her as you would do me."

They grunted, their sharp gazes taking me in.

"These males are Finsteg and Pulost," he said. "They'll rotate guarding me, though they'll be my primary security."

"Did Dakur have guards?"

"He shouldn't have needed them. He went to ensure a friend's vox was ready to leave." He explained how the orc prince and his mate had stopped here while traveling toward the orc kingdom, how they'd flown on a vox who was injured and visited with the Matis Clan while the vox healed.

"Was his mate orc or human?" It couldn't be her, could it? It would be too much of a coincidence, but there weren't many human women among the orcs.

"His mate is called Lyneth."

"We left the village at the same time," I said with excitement. "Was she safe? Healthy? She bonded with an orc mate as well?"

"Madr loves her above all others. Lyneth was well. They secured their bond. Unfortunately, when Dakur went to prepare their vox to travel, something horrible happened. We found a lot of blood and both he and the vox gone."

How could the thieves steal someone this far into the Matis Clan territory?

"I'm not sure what a vox is."

"A winged creature. Some orcs travel to the Ember Clan, who foster the voxes. When the young vox slips from its seed, it bonds with whoever is closest. Orcs wait for the chance to be chosen, though none of us in the Matis Clan have done this. We travel through the tree-tops by vine and the might of our arms. We've never felt the need to fly."

"And you're saying Lyneth flew on one of the voxes?"

He nodded. "When they landed, she appeared quite comfortable with the vox—and Madr. Know that he loved her and she him. When they left on one of our shaydes, she was safe and happy." He explained that they'd needed to rush back to the orc kingdom to be with Madr's father.

"So much happened to her from the time we parted in the forest," I said.

"To you as well."

I chuckled. "You know what?"

"What, my precious mate?" He cupped my face, and I was reminded all over again why I adored him. He was gentle and kind. Knowing he cared for me meant everything.

"One, I'm not as scared as I was when we landed on this platform, though I'm not yet ready to look down over the edge. And two, I'm going to be strong for you, Zickar. This I promise."

"You're already strong, mate. Never doubt that. You looked back at your past and scorned it. Not only that, but you also made decisions for your future without allowing your past to creep in and retake control."

How could he see all this in me when I could barely feel it myself?

"I know you," he said as if he could read my mind.

"You don't see like Tenkaril, do you?"

He laughed. "I'm no elder."

"I suspect you will be one day."

And I'd be there with him, holding his hand and making sure he knew how deeply he was loved.

With Finsteg in the lead and Pulost following, we walked to the edge of the platform.

Finsteg lifted his pendant and blew across it, a

gesture they seemed to use to command the vines. A bunch of them snapped down from the tree a short distance away, landing on the edge of the platform and securing their tips around it. Others joined the first, forming a slight mesh across the base, plus two stretched taut to provide handholds.

"We'll cross," Zickar told me. "Would you like me to carry you?"

I gulped. "It's . . . It's . . . We'll be able to see the ground far, far below us." How in the world was I going to do this?

"You'll only see it if you look down. If I carry you, you can look up."

"All right, I'll . . ." I scrunched my brow and stiffened my back. "Actually, no. I won't ask you to carry me. I'm going to walk with you. Please lead the way."

He gave me a skeptical look. Did he think I'd become so frightened I'd freeze on the platform?

Frankly, the thought had occurred to me already, and I'd decided I couldn't do it.

No, I *wouldn't* do it.

I wanted not only to fit in here, but I also wanted to make myself proud. He was right; I'd taken a huge step into a future I'd never imagined. How could I let myself slide back to the easily frightened person I was before?

"How do we cross?" I asked pleasantly, striding over to the vine bridge. I even looked down, though I gulped, and my heart flipped over.

An orc was walking on a trail below with a haunch of

something he'd killed draped across his shoulder. He glanced up, and when he waved, I did too.

I could do this.

Zickar had only taken a few steps, using the higher vines to hold his balance while placing his feet carefully on the mesh of vines spanning the bottom of the bridge. "Like this," he said, demonstrating stepping forward slowly, gripping the upper vines. He gave me a smile that made my insides start swirling around. I knew that expression in his eyes.

He was proud that I was going to challenge this fear. He was glad I was his mate. And he wanted to take me somewhere quiet where we could escape the world with each other.

I wanted this, too, though I had a feeling it would be some time before we'd be alone for that.

It was all right. We had a lifetime together for love.

I gripped the upper vine on my right, grateful to find it steady, and stepped out onto the mesh. It gave subtly beneath my shoes, but it felt sturdy enough. The vines had responded to Finsteg's pendant. Would they react to someone else's and snap away in a different direction while we walked across them?

This was not the time to be thinking about something like that.

Swallowing hard, I gripped the left, chest-high vine, and made my other foot join the first on the bridge.

Then I continued, following Zickar. As I moved, I did as he originally suggested, looked toward our destination—another large platform built around an enormous tree. I only glanced down when I needed to step, and I kept my focus then on the mesh itself, not the ground far below.

By the time I was halfway across, sweat was trickling down my temples, and my jaw ached from clenching my teeth together, but I was doing all right. I kept moving, and I hadn't frozen—yet.

A flock of birds swooped down, coming closer and closer, but I didn't have any food, so I dragged my gaze away from them.

One smacked into the side of my head, knocking me against the railing.

"Ah!" I wrapped both of my arms around the vine on my left and clung, gaping at the ground.

The birds flew past me, continuing on as if they didn't realize they'd nearly knocked me off the bridge.

Zickar held out his hand, and while I was desperate to take his comfort and help, I had to do this myself or I'd balk at everything that was flung my way in the future. How could I stand proudly by his side when I couldn't remain upright on my own two feet?

I growled and reached out to latch onto the other vine, using it to right myself on the bridge.

Pulost grunted. "Good."

A male of few—*one*—word.

Finsteg, a male of even fewer words shot me a smile that held a touch of approval.

"The fates chose well," he finally said, turning to continue across the bridge.

Zickar's eyes gleamed with humor, and that was enough to loosen my muscles. I started walking again.

The second half of the bridge went quickly. At this point, other than watching for another flock of birds, it almost felt simple. Like, I could get a pendant (did females get them too?) blow across it, and stride confidentially along my own vine bridge.

Ha ha. Not yet.

When we reached the other platform, I took Zickar's hand, and he led me around the enormous tree, passing homes built on the inside of the open deck. Finsteg and Pulost stopped at the last building in the row and Zickar opened the door, gesturing for me to enter ahead of him.

I'd started inside when a loud rumble rang out in the distance. Thunder?

Zickar's concerned gaze met the other male's, and Finsteg sucked in a deep breath before releasing it.

"We had trouble while you were gone," he said.

Zickar stepped back outside. "What kind of trouble?"

"Humans from afar have come to this area. Human females."

"I see," Zickar said with a frown.

"There's not a male among them."

That was odd.

"Are they moving into the closest village?" Zickar must mean my village built behind the high fortress wall.

"They arrived from a different direction," Pulost said. He waved to his left. "They crossed the desert, seeking a new home."

"Then they can build a fortress like the others," Zickar said carefully. "Negotiate a treaty with the orc kingdom if they feel in need of protection from the shaydes."

"They don't want to do that," Finsteg said.

"What do they want instead?" Zickar asked, peering in that direction.

"They're knocking down our trees." The words burst from Pulost. "And they're using the lumber to build their homes. Many homes."

CHAPTER 30
ZICKAR

A touch of dread shot through me, and I stepped to the edge of the platform, closed my eyes, and clutched my pendant. I listened to the whispers.

The trees didn't speak with us directly; we heard their emotions in the wind swirling through their leaves, the creaks of their branches, and when we touched them.

I sensed worry. Distress.

And pain.

A growl ripped through me, and if those harming our beloved trees were near, I'd slice them apart.

But I couldn't start a war until I had all the facts.

I needed more information and then I could form a plan. Turning, I crossed back over to Pulost and Finsteg. Alwen watched me with concern and a touch of wonder.

"How far away are the humans building their homes?" I asked.

"Within our forest," Finsteg snarled. "They're using our trees. Live ones!"

"They're too close," Pulost said. "They're encroaching on our territory already and when one of us spoke with their leader, she laughed and stated they would do whatever they pleased."

"They don't fear us or the shaydes. Not enough, anyway."

Finsteg gave me a sly grin. "Oh, I believe they fear the shaydes. The ashenclaws too. They've had a few unfortunate encounters with both."

"Enough encounters to negotiate with us about the trees?" I asked.

He shrugged. "Hard to say. It's good you're back, though. I wish Dakur . . ." He sighed heavily. "It's good you're back. You've been missed, and you'll soon set this right."

This must be the issue Tenkaril alluded to.

"What does all this mean?" Alwen asked.

"I don't have all the details yet, but I'm going to find out."

"Have humans ever moved into your clan's territory?" She leaned against my side.

"Never before. They usually fear us too much to come close."

"What will you do?"

"Talk to Tenkaril and the other elders. Learn all I can about the settlement and what their plans might be. And then I'll speak with them myself."

"They're not friendly," Pulost said with a sneer. "They feel as if they can cut down our trees and use the carcasses to build homes. They're burning some! They must be stopped."

"We've always known that others might choose to live near our clan's territory. We don't own the trees or the world around us. We've built homes high in the trees because they allow us to live among them. The fates might have a solution to this problem."

Finsteg grunted. "This isn't something the fates can decide."

"I'll always consult them, but you're correct. Whatever decision we come to must be reached with all the clan's input, not just mine or Tenkaril's."

The two males nodded.

"Let's go inside," I said with a touch of sadness.

Finsteg and Pulost strode over to stand on either side of the door, facing the forest with their weapons in hand. I urged Alwen inside and shut the door. When I blew across my pendant, a low hum rang out, and whisps in small chambers mounted near the ceiling gleamed.

"Welcome home, mate," I said.

CHAPTER 31
ALWEN

I took in the small entry room with wooden walls and two benches along the sides, plus the arched entrance leading to a larger room where whisps also glowed.

"You've built into the tree itself," I said in awe, striding in that direction. "Doesn't that cause the tree harm?"

"Not this variety. It thrives when we live within its trunk."

In the next room, I found a living area with comfortable appearing furniture, plus two rooms leading off it on either side. Peeking into the first, I found a bathing chamber, and in the other, an enormous bed fit for at least two orcs.

"The trees welcome us," he said.

"Would they welcome the women?"

He shrugged. "I don't know. If they're cutting down live trees, I'd say no."

"You built everything from dead trees?"

"Other than when we build inside their trunks, we use dead trees. The live ones speak to us, though only with impressions and emotions. The humans are harming them, and they're in distress. They're a part of us; a part of our clan. We'd no more kill them than we would each other."

"Maybe the women don't realize what they're doing," I said. "We cut trees for wood to burn during the cold months and for lumber to construct our homes. If they've moved to this area, they would do the same." I frowned. "Are all trees like the woods in this forest, beings who speak to you with emotions?"

"Many are, though not all."

To think we'd so easily chopped them down, burned them. My belly churned at the thought of harming another. When I hunted, it was to provide food I needed to survive. I'd done the same when I cut trees, but if I'd known, I would've taken only the dead wood lying on the forest floor.

"We need to stop them," I said fiercely. "I'll help if I can."

He tugged me into his arms and held me, curling forward to rest his chin on the top of my head. "I'm grateful I have you in my life."

"We'll find a way through this together."

"We will."

But I had to wonder how that was even possible.

We ate, bathed, and dressed, me in a skirt and top someone had neatly folded and placed on a chair in our bedroom.

"Other clothing will be made for you, and it'll fit better," Zickar said, smiling while I knotted a strip of cloth around my waist to hold up the skirt.

"Who makes your cloth?" I asked, studying the tiny weave and admiring the tight stitches. Someone had worked hard to make this outfit.

"In some of the meadows, we grow long rows of a plant that produces a soft fluff. That's twisted into thread that's used to weave into cloth. Others cut and stitch together our shirts, pants, and skirts. Blankets and coats for when it gets cold. We all produce as we're able, and many enjoy crafting such things."

"And the color?" I ran my fingertips down the dark purple skirt and plucked at the lighter lavender blouse with puffy sleeves and a rounded neckline.

"Some of our trees produce flowers in these colors. We use their petals to make a dye for the pale cream fluff we make into fabric."

"It's amazing. I'd love to see where they work someday."

"I'll take you there myself."

He wore a clean, simple cloth loincloth, this one dyed a dark green that contrasted nicely with his golden green skin.

We left our treetop home and descended to the

ground where we joined others walking down the wide trail to the teegars that would take us to where we'd celebrate Dakur's life.

Taking turns on the teegars, we shot below the ground and stepped out into an enormous cavern with falls on one side, a large pool filled with pale lavender water, and lush purple and green vegetation. Whisps sparkled like stars across the ceiling, generating enough light to see everything. We made our way to the central area where elders sat in chairs carved from large boulders. The chairs had been mounted on a raised half circle. They looked down on us solemnly as we settled on the wide, smooth ledges half an orc's height above the water.

With the trickly falls accompanying them, the orcs around me lifted their pendants and blew softly across them, creating a haunting melody that echoed in the enormous room.

Goodbye friend, someone cried out.

Others joined in, their voices blending with the mournful music.

May your path be ever easy, beloved caedos.

We'll miss you, Dakur.

Then they bowed their heads, and I did too. A few orcs sniffed and shed tears. Others outright wailed.

Tenkaril stared forward stoically, only the subtle tremble of her lower lip showed how much she mourned the loss of her son.

The sound of the water soothed my soul. Did the others feel it too?

Zickar squeezed my hand, and I leaned into his side.

After the moment of silence, we all rose. Someone started pouring a drink from one of many large jugs, and another handed us full cups. We lifted our drinks into the air, and I was astonished to see the sadness leave everyone as if they shed it like a wet cloak, to see smiles take its place.

"He was a good friend," Zickar shouted. "A brother unlike any other." He drank from his glass, as did I. The lightly sweet liquid slid down my throat.

"Yes," someone cried, lifting their drink again before taking a sip. "Dakur! The best!"

Others joined in hailing Dakur, and soon, low laughter rang out as orcs shared what they loved most about their former caedos. He'd been kind, a fearless warrior, and a strong leader.

He'd adored orclings and more than once, played games with them.

He'd sometimes worked in the gardens, stating there was nothing better than sinking his fingers into the soil.

He'd had a wonderful singing voice.

Once the voices grew silent, and we'd nearly finished our drinks, Tenkaril stood and lifted her glass. "To our new caedos, Zickar. May he lead wisely, kindly, and for a very long time."

We all drained the rest of the liquid in our cups.

Someone started beating on a drum, and soon,

everyone was dancing. It was somewhat feverish, yet poignant, as if everyone was bridging their mourning into hope for a better future.

I hadn't known Dakur, but even I cried. I laughed. I celebrated that he'd lived.

Zickar and I danced, then Pulost swung me away, followed by Finsteg. They took turns, stepping back to guard Zickar as if they thought someone might jump him. Surely no one would attack us here. How would they find us?

I spun and dipped so fast, my bare feet pounding the stone, that I became winded.

Zickar scooped me up and spun me around, making me laugh, making me dizzy. I noted other males lifting their mates, carrying them away from the crowd.

"I need you, love," Zickar whispered in my ear. "We've mourned our friend, but now we must celebrate life."

"Take me home, mate," I said. "I need you too."

He strode across the ledge, nodding to those we passed. They patted his arm, mine, too, and smiled, murmuring how glad they were that he was back, how happy they were to have me in their clan.

The humans I'd lived with had found me strange because I wore pants and hunted. Many had scorned me.

Here, I was welcome no matter what I wore.

We rode a teegar to the surface, then another projected us up to the first platform. This time, Zickar carried me across the vine bridge with Pulost leading and Finsteg following, their weapons ready to defend us.

They took their spots outside Zickar's door again as he carried me inside and locked the panel behind him.

Then he continued to our bedroom where he placed me on my feet and gently helped me remove my clothing. When we were naked, he lifted me again and reverently laid me on our bed.

"Mate," he said with a sigh full of need. "My pretty maiden."

CHAPTER 32
ZICKAR

I'd heard that humans mourned for a long time after the death of family or a friend, and we orcs did as well.

But we also celebrated. A life well lived, even if too short, was a blessing. I was grateful I'd been able to praise Dakur's life with my friends.

But being with Alwen would make me feel complete once more.

We didn't say anything to each other; we didn't need to. Each touch and each time our eyes met told us everything we needed to know. We were together, and the world could do what it willed. Whatever it threw our way, we'd face it side by side.

I kissed her, drinking from her lips, my sighs of pleasure echoed by hers. I wove my fingers through hers and held her hand above her head, bracing myself on my knees and elbow while I traced my fingertips down her body with my other hand. She pressed her breast into my hand, and I cupped it, running my thumb back and forth across the nipple. When I kissed down her neck and across her chest, she arched her spine, eager for my touch.

I kissed my way down to her nipple and sucked it into my mouth.

Fire kept bursting through me then backing off, coiling tight. My cock throbbed, and I couldn't wait to be with her once more. She was my life, my world, and everything I hadn't done enough to deserve.

Yet I was grateful to the fates for giving her to me.

We'd already been together, but this felt new. So precious. As I slid my fingers between her legs, groaning at how wet she was already, I wanted to focus on this moment. Every second, every touch mattered. We never knew what life would hand us next, so we had to hold onto what we had at this very moment.

Mate.

"I want to be with you," she whispered.

A growl ripped through me, the vibration transferring from my mouth to her nipple.

As I stroked her clit and rolled it between my finger and thumb, I looked up, savoring the rapture on her face.

"This feels good?" I asked.

"It's wonderful. Don't stop."

I smiled, and she did the same.

Precious mate. Pretty maiden. She was my life. My

world. I'd sacrifice everything to see her this happy every day of her life.

"I won't," I said. "I'm yours now, tomorrow, and for always."

"Mate," she said softly. "Glorious mate."

I flicked my tongue across her nipple, grinning when her gasp rang out. Could this get any better?

As I rubbed her clit, she bucked up against my hand.

"More," she sighed.

I slid a finger inside her. So tight. So wet and hot. I nearly came at how amazing she felt. Her response to my touch made my heart pinch tight.

Emotions beyond words roared through me. I'd never felt this way for anyone else, and if I died tomorrow, I'd have this time with Alwen. That's how vital being with her and loving her was for me.

"You're the loveliest person I know," I said, sliding my gaze down her body to watch as she thrust her hips up to meet my fingers. My thumb continued to rub her clit, and the whimpers of need she released made my cock smack against my abs.

"I need you," she cried. "Please."

I kissed down her belly and spread her thighs wider. When she hitched her legs onto my shoulders, I growled with satisfaction. Then I sucked her clit into my mouth, gently rolling it with my teeth while plunging my fingers inside her wet passage.

Her hips jerked up, and a moan ripped from her

throat. She clung to my horns, tugging on them and pulling my head closer to her body.

"I want all of you," she cried out. "Please."

Soon, mate. Soon. She was so sweet. I'd never tasted anything better, but like her, I needed more.

"Come for me," I growled. "Let me feel it on my mouth."

She lifted her hips, her gasps ringing out in the room. And then she splintered, crying out as her body quivered beneath me.

"Mate," I sighed. "You're beautiful."

My need was insatiable, my cock a thick staff flush against my abs.

I gently rolled her over and helped her onto her knees. "Is this all right?"

"Perfect." She looked back at me with complete trust, and if I died this instant, I'd still feel complete. Knowing she trusted me to keep her safe, to love her, was all I needed.

My cock insisted there was more.

I held her hips and slowly slid inside her, nearly coming because she was tight and wet. She pushed back, moaning into the bedding.

As I began to move inside her, my cock grew stiffer.

She bucked back to meet me, whimpering. "More, Zickar. Always more, my love, my mate."

As I moved faster, she ground against me, and our soft cries echoed in the room.

"Take your pleasure, love," I hissed. "Let me feel you come around my cock now."

"Yes," she moaned. "Yes."

Leaning over her, I stroked her breasts, tugging on her nipples. I trailed my fingertips across her belly and rubbed her clit.

She gasped and pushed back hard to meet my thrusts.

With a growl, I went faster, riding her while her body shivered, and she whimpered into the blankets. Her body crested through one surge after another. And when her spine loosened, and she started to slump on the bed, I shot my seed inside her, barking out my pleasure.

We fell to the bed, and I held her as I rolled us onto our sides.

"Zickar," she said, her voice soft and sweet. "I love you."

"Mate," I said, curling my body around hers, holding her tight.

She stroked my arm and melted against my chest.

Memories of Dakur rushed through me, and tears smarted behind my eyes. Us running through the woods, swimming in the river and collecting berries for Tenkaril to turn into jelly. Sitting with our clan for a fine meal, laughing as we argued over which cut of meat or which tuber was better. The time I broke my leg, and he helped me back to our clan, then stood with me while the healers reset my leg.

I was going to miss him; there was no doubt about

that. I'd do all I could to be the best caedos possible. That was why he'd chosen me as his second, because he knew if something happened, I'd protect our clan like we'd defended each other.

"You're sad," she said, and when she sniffed, I knew she cried too. She hadn't met Dakur, but she knew him from the tales we'd shared tonight and from the respect we all showed to his memory.

That was the reason we gathered, that we celebrated.

I'd lost my best friend, but I had my mate.

And that would be enough.

CHAPTER 33
ALWEN

The next day, Zickar met with the elders to discuss the human situation and catch up on the caedos duties he would now need to handle.

While I was puttering around inside our home, trying to decide what I could do to help my new clan, someone knocked on the door. I opened it to find an orc woman standing on the platform, dressed in a skirt and blouse.

She gave me a shy smile. "I'm Sessavia. Zickar asked me to show you around and help you feel more settled here."

"Wonderful. I'm Alwen."

"It's nice to meet you, Alwen. Why don't we begin our day together with breakfast?" My belly growled at her words, and she laughed. "A good plan, then, right?"

"Right." I'd looked around in our home but hadn't found any food. They ate. I just didn't know where.

I stepped out onto the platform and shut the door. There didn't appear to be a way to lock it, and I mentioned the fact.

"Why would you need to lock your door?" Sessavia asked with a low laugh, something she seemed to do often in addition to smiling. It was contagious, and I kept smiling back.

"To keep people from . . ." Would it be impolite to suggest someone in our clan might rob us?

"Ah," she said. "You worry someone will claim your home while you're away?"

"Oh, um, no, not that. I—"

"No one would ever take your home from you. Zickar is our caedos and you, as his mate, are equally respected."

"I should have to earn respect."

"You are wise." She waved to the left side of the platform, and we walked in that direction, stopping at an opening in the rail. "Some in our clan may wait to get to know you before deciding, but most of us accept you because the fates chose you for our caedos."

"What I mean was that we keep our personal possessions inside our home."

"I've heard that humans sometimes take things they shouldn't, that they make claims on possessions that are not their own."

"Yes. Thievery is too common in my village."

"Sad, isn't it?" She sighed and lifted her pendant that

looked much like Zickar's, a five-point star. "You won't need to worry about such things here. No one would think of entering your home if you weren't there or without permission, and the thought of someone taking your belongings is unheard of. No one owns anything. Yes, we have clothing made that fits us best, but if we need more, it is readily given to us. Why would anyone need to take yours when they could obtain more just by asking?"

She blew softly across her pendant and vines snapped down from a tree some distance away from us.

"Do you exchange money for items you need?" I asked, following her across the bridge. My guts lurched a bit when I looked down, but not as badly as the day before. I was getting used to this, settling into my home, and the thought made me proud.

"We exchange one service for another. Each contributes as they're able."

"What if someone doesn't want to work?"

She paused at the end of the bridge before stepping onto another, bigger platform. "Why wouldn't they?"

Did this mean no one here was lazy?

Without waiting for my answer, she walked across the open area between the vine bridge and a single, large building built completely around an enormous tree.

"Everyone contributes in one way or another," she said. "We're happy to do this to benefit our clan."

"This sounds wonderful."

"It truly is." Her gaze glided down my front, but I didn't sense judgment. More that she was assessing me. "What skills do you have?"

"When I lived in the village, I hunted for my family."

"You could help our hunters, then. But we'll decide this over the next week or so. You may have other skills we need more, skills that will benefit your mate, our new caedos."

I wasn't sure what that might be. I wouldn't lounge around waiting for others to take care of me, however. I was going to contribute in any way I could.

She opened the door to the large building and waved for me to enter ahead of her, following me inside. "You're certainly welcome to have meals in your own home. Some do, and food will be provided. But most of us gather with the clan and eat whenever we're hungry."

We joined a short line of orcs moving toward an open window. A male stood inside a room in the back, greeting each person by name. When he saw me, his eyes widened, as did his smile.

"Welcome," he said, dipping his head forward.

"I'm Alwen."

"Welcome, Zickar's mate. I'm Brudon."

"It's nice to meet you, Brudon." I hoped I'd soon be known for who I was and not just for who I was associated with. Funny how I hadn't cared about building my identity while living in the village. I'd done my best to remain hidden, especially after what happened. Naturally, I did what I must to support my family, though there was never enough.

My heart pinched at the thought. Was my mother finding a way to get by? My brother must be hunting. Perhaps he was working with the butcher as well. Was he happy?

And my sisters. They were so young and innocent. I'd hated to leave them to whatever fate the village dealt them.

Could I find a way to help them? I'd talk to Zickar about it tonight. He mentioned something about—

Brudon waved to a variety of food being offered. "What would you like, Alwen?"

I pointed, and he served me a generous portion, placing it on a wooden plate, and at my nod, adding a slice of bread and a blob of a dark lavender jelly.

"Here you are. Enjoy." He handed me the plate and looked to Sessavia, who also ordered her food while I waited.

We sat at a wooden table with benches lining both sides, half full of orcs talking as they ate. Laughter rang out in the room and while there were only a few orclings present, everyone appeared happy.

"I can't imagine living in a place where everyone's welcome," I said, sitting and putting my plate on the wooden surface in front of me.

Sessavia settled beside me. "Why not?"

"It's . . ."

"Not the way of humans?" When I didn't speak, she frowned. "I apologize if I've offended you. I don't know much about humans, only what I've been told by others who've encountered them."

"The Matis Clan doesn't participate in the mate hunt?"

"Not so far, which is why many were surprised to find you with Zickar. The fates find a way, don't they?"

"They do."

We ate, and everything tasted fresh and wonderful.

Zickar joined us partway through our meal, lowering his plate beside mine and settling on the bench.

His two guards also got food but sat near the door, facing Zickar to watch him.

He kissed my temple and gave me a warm smile, including Sessavia in his grin. "How are things going, Alwen?"

"Well, Sessavia's showing me around. I thought it would be nice to visit the Flazant family if that's all right." The latter, I directed to Sessavia, who nodded.

"I'm glad you're settling in," he said, taking a big bite of bread, ripping through it with his tusks and chewing.

"I'll stop at the smithy to get her a pendant first," Sessavia said. "Then I can begin teaching her our clan's language."

"Language?" I asked, looking between them both. Everyone I'd met spoke universal.

"I mean the language of our clan's pendants," she

said. "You want to learn how to call your own bridges, right?"

"Yes, that would be great." Would vines actually listen if I blew across a piece of metal? I couldn't wait to find out. "What will you be doing today, Zickar?"

He frowned, and his hand paused while lifting food to his mouth. "I'm going to go to the edge of the forest and see what the humans are doing."

"I can come with you."

He placed his hand over mine where it sat on the table. "Not yet, though I may have need of you, mate. Take today to learn your way around the central clan area. Visit the Flazants and get your pendant. We can talk about what I learn at the human village tonight."

"Be careful." I wasn't sure why I said it. The women building on the edge of the forest wouldn't try to harm him, would they? My village had formed a truce with the orcs. We needed them as much as they needed us— though our only contribution was mates. Surely all humans felt the same.

"I will."

We took our empty plates to another counter where an orc male cheerfully took them for washing, and left the dining building, pausing outside. Pulost and Finsteg remained close by. Seeing them reminded me that they'd be with Zickar, a reassuring thought. They'd keep him safe.

As if he read my mind, Finsteg nodded, his flinty gaze sliding from mine to assess the area around us.

"I'll see you tonight?" Zickar asked.

I nodded, feeling strangely melancholy, though I wasn't sure why. I knew when we reached his clan that he'd be busy, that we wouldn't spend all our time together, so that couldn't be it.

Perhaps it was because things were changing for the orcs and our clan. With humans settling nearby and the Flazants coming for their young, our world might be different moving forward. I wasn't responsible for doing anything about this, but I still felt as if I needed to be involved in what happened. A silly thought when I'd hunted and stayed inside with my family while living in the village. I'd barely paid any attention to what the mayor or anyone else was doing.

Zickar lifted me up and kissed me, his mouth lingering on mine. I wanted to drag him back to our home, to disappear into our bedroom forever, but the clan needed him. With reluctance, I released him and gave him a reassuring smile.

"I'll see you tonight," I said, keeping my voice neutral. I wasn't going to worry about him until I had just cause.

But my heart thudded quickly as he stroked my cheek, turned away, and leaped off the platform, landing squarely on the branch of another tree.

"This way." Sessavia took my arm and guided me to the opposite edge of the platform. She called a teegar, and we descended to the ground.

"Why do they project us if they can smoothly rise up and hover beside the platform?"

"Because it's fun when they shoot us into the air."

That was a matter of perspective.

"I've noticed all the orcs leap off the platforms." I felt deficient in this as well.

"I don't believe you can, though, right?"

I shook my head. "The distance is too great. I'd get hurt."

"We have teegars, and they're well fed and happy. They'll take you to the ground and bring you back up to the platforms without a single protest."

"Once I learn how to call them."

She gave me an understanding smile and rubbed my arm. "Which is why we'll get your pendant as soon as possible. Then I'll show you how to produce some basic commands."

"Thank you," I said as the teegar stopped at the ground level and we stepped off. "I don't know what I'd do without you."

Her bright laugh rang out. "You're stronger than you believe, Alwen. You'd find a way."

We walked along a trail through the woods, stopping at a stone building where a big burly orc worked with metal. A fire roared in the center of a large open room and sweat drizzled down his back as he lifted a hammer and brought it down hard on a glowing piece of metal.

"He doesn't do this in the canopy for obvious reasons," Sessavia said as we waited for him to finish what he was doing. "His work is loud. And we don't want to bring fire near the trees."

The ground beneath his building was made up of huge slabs of flat ledge, and they'd extended stone well beyond the building. If a spark escaped his work, it could be quickly stamped out without causing damage.

Once he'd finished what he was working on, the orc came over to join us, nodding both to Sessavia and me.

"Alwen is Zickar's mate, and she needs a pendant," Sessavia said. "This is Ulong. He's an expert metalworker."

I nodded and gave him a smile.

His gaze remained sober, though he dipped his head forward once. "Let me see what I have."

"He's grumpy," Sessavia said softly as Ulong stepped back into his shop.

"I heard that," he growled. "And I'm not grumpy. I'm busy. Serious. As an orc should be."

She grinned and lowered her voice even further. "*Really* grumpy."

"And I heard that." He stomped back out of his shop holding a basket that he held out to me. "Pick one."

"Please," Sessavia said with a smirk.

He scowled at her and nudged the basket my way again.

I peered inside, studying the pendants. "They all look the same."

"They're not, obviously," he said. "And I don't just

mean by the metal and the work it took to make each special."

"The fates will help you choose the unique pendant that's been made for you," Sessavia said. "That's what this grumpy male means."

He growled.

Interesting. I studied the pendants closely. Yes, they were all similar, but there were subtle differences. A tiny scratch along one point of a star. A little blemish in the center. Another had a roughness to the underside.

"If they're all a bit different, how do they work consistently?" I asked.

"A good question," Ulong said, his gaze cutting to Sessavia. "See? Our caedos's new mate is wise."

Sessavia huffed and matched his scowl.

"Oh, um . . ." I didn't want to be the source of a squabble between them.

"*I'm* also wise," she said.

"That remains to be seen." Ulong's attention returned to me.

She snapped her tusks together.

He ignored her. "Have you chosen?" he asked me.

I felt them all again, but one warmed to my touch.

"Can I take this one?" I lifted the one with the tiny circular blemish in the center.

"Yes. Excellent choice."

I held it up in the light.

"We have leather strands you can use to wear it," he

added, shooting Sessavia a look I'd take as longing if they hadn't just been arguing.

Oh . . . So it was like that, was it?

Sessavia took a strip of leather and helped me string the pendant, securing it around my neck.

I looked down at it with pride and excitement.

For the first time in what felt like forever, I felt as if I belonged.

I traveled through the treetops with Pulost in the lead and Finsteg behind. I didn't want or need guards, but I could occasionally see their value. If I tried to dismiss them, Tenkaril would snarl. I wasn't worried about that so much as I didn't want her to worry. She'd lost one son. If they were with me, there was less chance she'd lose another.

The forest in this part of our world was so vast, it would take days to travel it even by winged vox. On foot, it took much longer. But the vines knew us. They lived in harmony with the trees like us. So with a few bursts of air across our pendants, they swung up to meet us as we moved through the canopy.

Still, it took hours to reach the western side of the forest. The sea and the orc kingdom could be found on the opposite side of the vast woods and eastward, and the Ember Clan claimed the vast desert in the southern region of this continent. A migratory people; they traveled from one oasis to another, living in temporary structures they could assemble or take down almost in minutes.

Mountains covered the area to the north of us, and the human village that had made a treaty with the orcs to exchange protection for mates had been built in the foothills. Trees grew along the slopes, but that variety was stubby and scraggly due to the soil. They weren't enormous and sentient like the ones in my clan's part of the world.

I slowed my pace as I approached the edge of the forest. My plan was to observe, not interact with the humans.

Landing squarely on a branch of one of *our* trees, I waited for Finsteg to join me and Pulost. We squatted on our haunches and peered through the canopy toward the village being slowly constructed between the edge of the woods and the first slope of a lower western mountain.

They'd taken down at least ten trees. A very loud device had been set up near the woods and women hefted big spans of trunk onto the device, pushing it toward a large metal blade that sliced through it like the sharpest of knives. Slabs fell to each side, and I could hear the keening cry of the tree as it was cut. Like I'd taken a blade through a limb, I pressed my hand to my chest. Tears smarted in the backs of my eyes.

They were torturing the living trees. Why not cut the

dead like we did? At least that tree's spirit had passed and wasn't aware of what happened with its carcass.

The trees around me whispered and moaned, mourning the loss of their sister.

"This is . . ." Pulost sent me a horrified look. "This is terrible. Don't you see? They must be stopped."

"How can they not realize what they're doing?" Finsteg asked, his hand on the hilt of his blade. "Surely, they must also hear the screams. We need to put a permanent end to this now."

"I agree," I said.

We were peaceful people, but when it came to protecting the clan—and the trees were part of the Matis clan—we could be ruthless.

"We can wait until night falls and attack," Pulost said grimly. "They'll be confused in the dark." He leaned forward as if he'd leap from the tree and begin the battle this instant.

"Under any other circumstances, I'd agree."

"What do you mean?" Finsteg shot a frown at me over his shoulder. "You agreed we must end this permanently."

"They're human. Even if they aren't part of Alwen's village, is it right for us to swoop in and kill them?"

Pulost snarled. "They've attacked our clan. We must protect our trees."

"I agree, and we will." But I hesitated before speaking of how we'd do this, something I never would've done in the past. Back then, the same fury would've filled me. I would've returned to the clan, explained, and a large group of us would've come back to attack. "I'm not sure their death is the answer. Not yet anyway."

Why did I wish to proceed at a slower pace?

"What must they do, attack *us*?" Pulost asked. He spit toward the ground, making his disgust with me clear. "I'll handle this if you've grown too soft too do this yourself."

My growl ripped out, and birds nesting above us squawked and scattered.

"Pulost," Finsteg warned. "You're not caedos. Give him time to think."

"There's no thinking needed." Pulost lowered his voice and lightened his tone, but anger darkened his face. "They're killing our trees and encroaching on our territory. If we permit this, they'll move in farther, cutting down more trees and building more structures. Before you know it, they'll be nesting right below us."

"I won't permit such a thing," I said firmly, irritated that he'd question me before I had a chance to speak my mind.

"Dakur never would've paused. He'd be firing arrows at them by now."

I stiffened. "I'm not my brother, but that doesn't mean I can't handle this in the best way possible."

"Enough, Pulost," Finsteg ground out. "This is not your decision to make." He turned to me, his face neutral, though his eyes watched me. Did he judge me as well?

"You killed those who murdered Dakur. How different is this situation versus that?"

"They murdered my brother," I snarled. "I made sure they'd never harm another."

"These females harm our trees who are our limbs, our clan, our sisters. How is this different?" he asked.

The canopy rustled above, and I sensed the trees also listened, perhaps judging me in the same way as my friends.

"We need to speak to the women," I said. "Tell them the harm they're causing. If they understand, they'll construct their buildings elsewhere. We may make allies out of them instead of enemies."

"Why do we need human allies?" Pulost asked.

"They sit on our western flank. Anything or anyone coming from this direction would need to pass them first. If we're allies, they'll notify us. Then we can be prepared for whatever might head our way."

"Wise," Finsteg said, his lips twitching upward. He elbowed Pulost. "See? Zickar is suggesting they could provide a buffer between the far west and this side of the forest. He's not suggesting we won't attack if these humans don't agree to our demands."

"In all honesty, I feel this is weak," Pulost said with dismay. He wasn't necessarily saying *I* was weak, but he was coming close. "Do you hesitate because they are your mate's people?"

"They're not of her clan." I didn't believe they were, that is.

Pulost shook his head. "If her brother tried to kill you, would you make the attempt to defend yourself or would you allow him to do it?"

"Of course I'd defend myself," I said, drawing myself up stiffly.

"Then do so now," Pulost said, pulling the blade from his side.

"You seem to think this is solely my decision to make. We must consult with the elders. I'm caedos, but I'm not a king who dictates to those around him. We come to decisions together."

"Tenkaril is old, blind," Pulost said carefully.

"She sees," Finsteg said, scowling at the other male. "Something you apparently don't."

"What I see are human females ripping through our precious trees and using their bones to construct houses. It hurts deep in my chest." He pressed his fist against the area above his heart. "They have no respect for the world around them."

"I'm finished with this conversation," I said. Frustrated with him and the unease I still felt, I leaped off the tree, landing squarely on the ground. While the two males hissed at each other behind me, I lifted my chin and strode from the forest and into the center of the newly built human village.

A cry rang out from one of the women.

She lifted a weapon unlike anything I'd ever seen before. Placing it against her mouth, she blew through it, shooting something at me.

CHAPTER 35
ALWEN

"Again," Sessavia said. "Close your eyes, make sure the angle is right, then gently blow across your pendant. Listen to the sound, feel the vibration you make in the tips of your fingers."

We'd been standing on the ground for over an hour on top of a teegar that was supposed to take us below the surface where we'd visit with the Flazants.

She told me I had to tell the teegar what we needed, that she wouldn't do it for me. So far, I'd been projected upward four times, shot sideways twice, and at least ten times, I swear it growled at me with disgust.

Sessavia patted my arm. "It takes practice."

"How long did it take for you to master this?"

"Master?" Her low laugh rang out, though I could tell she wasn't mocking me. "We're gifted with our pendants when we're young, and we practice together until we can almost create sounds in our sleep. But I'd say it took me months before the teegars always knew what I needed."

Then no one would expect me to be able to control the teegars in a few hours.

She frowned. "As for the teegar descend call, that's a simple one. I'd say I was able to create that sound the second or third time I tried."

I sighed. "I'm sorry."

"You weren't raised with our clan. It's natural for you to take more time. I'm sure the sound was solid in my mind before I lifted my pendant."

"How many different sounds can you make?"

"Thirty? Forty? I don't keep count. But when we discover a new sound, we share it with the clan."

"How do you find new sounds?"

"Wanderers do this for us. Dakur . . ." She pinched her eyes shut before opening them. "I understand when Dakur was young, he wanted to be a wanderer, but his path took him in a different direction. Wanderers are clan members who travel, trying out new sounds to see if anything in the world around us responds."

"Amazing."

"I heard Dakur was the best outside of those who learned this skill from elder wanderers, that he could make plants do almost anything. Someone told me once that he'd found a way to communicate with ashenclaws, though I have my doubts. How could that be true? No, it was someone who admired him greatly exaggerating his skill to impress me."

"I'm so sorry he's lost to our clan. I wish I could've done something for him."

"You were there. You bore witness. That has made a difference for my clan." She swallowed deeply. "Now try again." She nudged my pendant I still held in my hand. Coming around behind me, she placed her fingers over mine. "Your tilt isn't quite right. This is how you must do it. Don't blow across it yet. Close your eyes and try to feel the position first. Master that, and the wind will follow."

I hoped so. If I couldn't figure out how to create this simple sound, I'd be grounded. Or I'd be learning how to climb trees. For a woman who never wished to leave the ground, I suddenly wished that I could—as long as I was the one making it happen.

Closing my eyes, I memorized the angle I held my hand.

"Now blow," she said softly.

In my first attempt, I'd blown too hard, the second, not hard enough. I went back and forth after that.

I pulled in a breath and tried to feel the world around me, to sense how the teegar wished to be called. I pursed my lips and released a bit of air across my pendant.

We sunk below the surface.

"Well done," Sessavia said softly, her voice shifting with her light laugh. "Easy, right?"

"Yes," I breathed as the teegar came to a stop a few stories beneath the surface. "Easy." My laugh rang out. "We'll see how I do later when it's time for us to return to the surface."

We stepped off the teegar, and it shot upward.

"There are many entrances to this system of caverns," Sessavia said as we walked slowly down a wide tunnel with whisps glowing above and on the stone walls around us to light our way.

The tunnel opened into a large cavern with rows of homes built on top of each other along both sides. Mist drifted off a pool of water in the center, and I spied an orc sitting on the opposite bank, fishing. While we paused, he shouted in excitement then pulled in his line. He lifted a good-sized fish and shot us a smile.

"Looks like you caught dinner," Sessavia called out, waving for me to take the cobblestone path weaving between the small lake and the homes.

A few orclings played in front with indulgent parents sitting nearby, while others splashed in the shallow water on the shore. With so many whisps peppering the roof three stories above, it was as bright as day down here.

"This is amazing," I said. "I wasn't sure what to expect when I heard about people living below ground."

"It doesn't rain here," she said. "And there's very little wind. Fewer predators. Who wouldn't enjoy that?"

A shayde rushed from a tunnel ahead of us, and the orclings squealed with joy.

"That's not Taen." At least, I didn't think it was the shayde Zickar rode into the meadow, though I hadn't seen the beast for very long. "He had a bit of gold in his ruff."

"You're right," she said. "This is Millamay. She's the only female shayde in our clan. Her other brother is Noul. If I know him—" She nodded her head toward the tunnel. "See him hiding in the dark? He's waiting for her to think he's not following before he . . ."

Millamay had stopped by the shore and was drinking.

Noul burst from the passage and raced up behind her, tackling her. The two fell into the water, creating a big splash to the delight of the orclings playing nearby. The shaydes swam across the water, stepping out of the lake near where the orc was fishing. The male gave them both pats. The shaydes shook, scattering water, and the orc recoiled while laughing.

"This is a paradise," I said.

"It is wonderful." Pride shone in Sessavia's voice. "Come. We'll continue to the next cavern that's much different than this one. Many ecosystems are represented down here."

We walked into the tunnel Noul had left.

"How is that possible? Wouldn't they all be the same?"

She blew across her pendant, and a gust of wind flew through the passage. The whisps around us burst into light. "No one knows how this is possible, yet it is. Farther into the ground, you'll find caverns that are so cold, the water remains frozen all the time. We chip away at it and use the ice to keep our food cold. But in other directions, you'll find caverns full of swampland, others with crystals growing up from the ground, and some with lush vegetation. The air in those is hot and full of moisture."

"How without sunlight and rain?"

"Large whisps provide the light and water trickles onto the plants from above. When one of the wanderers was testing new sounds, she not only discovered that some of the plants enjoyed music, but she also found a large body of water above being fed by falls. The water very slowly makes its way through the thick area of stone, where it's filtered. Small channels have eroded over time, and the water eventually rains down on the plants."

We came to an intersection in the tunnel, and she gestured to the left. "This one slopes downward for many cliks. At the bottom, you'll find the cold caves. There are other, smaller caves along the sides of the passage, and some orcs live there when it's hot above ground. They love how cool it is."

"Do you?"

"I enjoy living in the canopy. The wind and the whisper of the trees soothes my soul."

"Where does Ulong live?"

"Oh, above ground as well. In the canopy. He has a home next to mine, and let me tell you, he snores. A few times, I've gotten up and stomped over to the wall between us and kicked it."

"Does that help?"

She laughed ruefully. "Unfortunately not."

"Maybe if you were lying in bed with him, you could nudge his side, and that would stop his snoring."

She gasped. "Who would ever want to lie beside Ulong?"

"Oh, I imagine a lovely orc female might wish to lie with him." I waved to the channel on the right. "Where does that one go?"

"No female would ever want to be with Ulong," she snapped. "He's ornery, mean, and much too grumpy."

"I'm sure some might find that attractive."

"I can't imagine who."

"I wonder if Ulong will find her. Does he go to the hunt?"

"He has not." She huffed. "No woman would ever agree to mate with him."

"A big, burly orc like him? He's dripping muscles, and he has a good job. I'm sure he could provide well for a female."

Pinching her eyes shut, she shook her head. "No, no one will want him."

"What would you do if someone did?"

"I'd rip his head off and feed it to him." She stomped forward. "As for the right tunnel, that leads to the hot areas full of plants. Gardeners cultivate what we need, and we harvest regularly."

"I think that's wonderful. Down here, you're not subject to uncontrolled weather. Each area has its own special system that fits in with your clan's life."

"That's correct." Urging me to walk with her, we

continued going straight. "As for Ulong, he will *not* be going to the hunt."

"What's stopping him? Are there rules about who can participate?"

"Only those imposed by our clan's fates, but we don't send anyone to the hunt yet. Dakur had talked about going, however, so perhaps some will next year."

"Maybe the fates will select Ulong."

"They'd better not," she growled, stomping ahead of me down the passage. "Come. The Flazants are this way."

Grinning, I followed. Maybe the next time I saw Ulong, we'd have a little chat.

For a woman who didn't think romance would ever be a part of her future, I was sure interested in matching others.

"Why did you choose this area for the Flazants?" I asked, walking beside her. I lifted my pendant and blew across it like she had, hoping to create the right sound to generate wind that would brighten the whisps, but it didn't work. In fact, water started dripping on us from above.

"It looks like you've discovered the sound to generate rain in this tunnel," she said with a smile. Lifting her pendant, she blew across it and the rain stopped. "I'd rather not get wet, however. As for the Flazants, I'll show you."

We walked for about half a clik, slowly moving downward. Light bloomed ahead, and it seemed as if the entire ceiling of the cavern we entered was covered with ignited whisps. Nearly blinded, I shielded my eyes.

That's when the heat hit me.

"They're living in a desert," I sighed with happiness. "The perfect place for my friends."

"Alwen," Trillie called out, her cry echoed by her sisters. They raced across the big open sandy area peppered with tall plants covered with spikes and launched themselves at me.

I would've fallen if Sessavia hadn't reached out and snatched me from their embrace, shifting me behind her.

"Gentle," she told the Flazant girls. "She's a fragile human." She shot me a grin. "Not a big brawny orc like me."

"Sorry, sorry," they cried. "Miss you."

Dillu made his way over to us at a slower pace, though his smile was just as blinding. He patted my arm, and I held in my wince.

Maybe I *was* a fragile human.

"How are you?" I asked them all.

"It wonderful here," Brillie said, glancing back over her shoulder. "We have plenty food and small pool on other side where we drink and bathe."

"We run. A lot," Trillie said. "Exercise important."

"It is." Because she sounded so serious about that, I pinched my lips together to keep from laughing.

"Me bored," Villadeer said, tugging on my arm. "Play wit us?"

My glance at Sessavia asked her if we had time, and she nodded.

"What kind of game can we play?" I asked, peering around. "I'm not sure seek and find will work here. The plants are too skinny." I tipped my head back, taking in the cave openings high along the walls. Small, dark purple birds dove in and out of them, chirping. "Wait, you said water?"

Villadeer nodded, her eyes gleaming with excitement.

"Can you take me there? I have an idea."

Trillie scooped me up and raced across the sand, her big feet slogging through it, sinking with each step. Brillie paced with us, squealing, and Villadeer trotted along so close behind, I worried she'd trip Trillie.

Sessavia smiled and came after us at a more sedate pace.

When we reached the edge of the oasis, Trillie put me down on my feet. I approached the clear pool full of pale purple water and studied the shore. Yes, this would work.

"I think we should build sand buildings," I said. "Sessavia will judge our creations, and whoever wins gets a prize."

Villadeer frowned, looking down at my hands. "What prize? No prize here."

"It's a special surprise," I said, stalling for time because I had no idea what I'd offer.

"It's a clan pendant," Sessavia said. "And I'll even teach you how to call the wind with it."

"Ahhh," the girls cried together.

Dillu joined us, though he chose to sit on a boulder near the broad pond and watch instead of competing.

We each took a section along the shore and started digging, scooping up sand to construct our structures.

"Time us?" I asked Sessavia.

She nodded. "An hour?"

"Perfect."

Since I had a pendant, and I'd thought up this game to make the girls happy, I didn't put much effort into my sculpture. The girls took it quite seriously, though, and added smooth stones, sticks and flowers they found in the pond, and even a few whisps they scraped off a nearby wall and mounted on the sides of their buildings to make them glow.

I swear, Villadeer had a knack for art, because her structure looked like a mythical castle.

"Time is over," Sessavia shouted, rising from the low rock where she'd sat while we worked. She hummed and frowned as she walked around each of our buildings, lifting her thick unibrow when she paused to study mine. She huffed and went over to stand with Dillu. They spoke in soft whispers, discussing our art. Well, she talked. Dillu nodded and smiled.

Finally, she grunted and turned our way. "And the winner is Villadeer!"

The little girl shrieked with joy and dashed around,

crowing about her win. Then she hurried over to stand in front of Sessavia. "Pendant. Pendant!"

"I'll have to speak to Ulong," Sessavia said, scowling. "And everyone knows how much I enjoy that. But I'll bring the basket of pendants here tomorrow, and you can choose one."

"Teach wind," Villadeer said, hopping around. "Wind!"

"Yes," Sessavia said with a smile. "I'll also teach you how to call wind."

We left the Flazants and strode through the tunnels.

Hearing shouts in the first cave, we picked up our pace, striding out into the open.

"There she is," someone yelled. "Alwen. Alwen! Zickar's been hurt."

My knees nearly gave out. "No." I rushed toward the crowd who'd gathered near the cave entrance. "Where is he? What happened?"

"He went to negotiate with the humans," someone said. "Damn them. How could they harm our caedos?"

"How badly is he hurt?" I asked, my belly lurching and my hands shaking.

"He's with the healers."

No, no, no.

I ran past them with Sessavia hurrying behind me. When I reached the end of the last tunnel, I made my way to the top.

It was only when I reached the ground level that I realized I'd called the teegar with my very first try.

CHAPTER 36

ZICKAR

Something small and sharp burst from the tip of the human's odd weapon. It hit me in the abdomen like the kick of a shayde. I groaned, falling to my knees.

As I tumbled to the ground, Pulost and Finsteg flung themselves from the trees, attacking the humans, driving them away from me.

"He lives," Finsteg growled, stooping at my side. "And that's the only reason I'm not killing them all."

"Get him out of here," Pulost said. "I'll make sure they don't do anything else."

Finsteg dragged me to the edge of the human village.

"I can walk," I snarled, my belly burning. As I pressed them against the wound, blood seeped around my fingers.

"Then rise to your feet," Finsteg said, one side of his brow lifting.

I couldn't make my legs work. They moved, but

despite trying to rise onto my feet, they wouldn't support my weight. Did humans use poison on their projectile weapons? If so, I'd be dead soon.

Finsteg grunted as he lifted me onto his shoulder. He ran into the woods with Pulost taking the rear, snarling and threatening the few women who dared follow. Rather than coming deeper into the woods, they backed away, sliding into their newly constructed homes.

I'd been foolish to enter their village. I should've remembered how Alwen described her people. They didn't trust orcs. I could've sent a missive announcing my arrival first.

My blood slithered down Finsteg's chest as he moved through the forest. He stuck to a trail initially before taking to the treetops where Pulost called vines ahead of us with his pendant.

"I can walk," I growled, and Finsteg lowered me onto a wide branch, keeping a hold on my arm until I proved I could bear my own weight. Blood trickled down my leg from the wound on my abdomen, and I swear I felt something sharp inside me. It bit into my innards each time I moved. But I wouldn't let Finsteg carry me the entire way. I had to do this on my own.

Ignoring my protests, he placed my arm across his shoulders, and while Pulost continued to call vines, Finsteg gave me support to walk from one tree to another.

By the time we reached the outskirts of my clan's territory, the sun hovered low on the horizon. My legs shook and it was all I could do to remain awake. My wound had continued to bleed, and my head pounded and spun.

"Call the healers," Pulost shouted the moment he spied the first guards. "Bring them to the caedos's home quickly."

The male grunted and called vines to swing through the trees, moving ahead of us.

Like he'd done the last few cliks, Pulost took my other arm. They urged me through the canopy. It was all I could do to stay on my feet.

By the time they reached the platform with my home, my vision had blurred, and they were dragging me.

Finsteg thrust open the door to my dwelling. He lifted and carried me inside, laying me gently on the bed.

"My son," Tenkaril cried, entering the outer room and hurrying into the bedroom with the help of her assistant. She sunk down onto the bed beside me and ran her fingers across my cheek. "What happened?"

Finsteg explained while Pulost sighed, clearly worried about me.

"We need the healers," Tenkaril snapped. "Get them immediately."

Pulost grunted. "They're on their way."

Within moments, three healers rushed into my home with their bags of medicine slung over their shoulders. They urged Tenkaril to sit in a nearby chair and hold my hand while they examined me.

"I've never seen anything like this before," one said with a mixture of awe and dismay. "What kind of weapon thrusts a metal object inside a person like this? There was no arrow?" This, he asked Finsteg.

It was all I could do not to pass out. My brain kept floating, taking me above my body, and my mouth had turned into a desert.

"Drink," I slurred.

"Get him water," Tenkaril said, her voice breaking. "He's thirsty. My poor son. Why didn't I see this either?"

One of the healers shook her head. "No water yet. Let us finish examining him first." Her gaze met mine. "We need to remove whatever they shot inside you before it does any further damage. I worry it will hurt to remove it, however."

"Do it," I grated out. "I'm fine."

I was anything but.

"Find his mate," Tenkaril said. "Alwen will want to be here."

I hated that my mate would worry. How had we gone from being happy and confident about our future, to this?

One of the healers cleansed a long, thin blade. She sprinkled a powder over my wound and wiped it away with a wet cloth, repeating the process three times. At least I'd stopped bleeding.

Why did my mind keep trying to leave my head? It was all I could do to keep it inside me.

"Hold him," a healer said. "Shoulders. Legs. Everyone."

With me braced to the bed, the healer bent over my abdomen.

"Zickar," Alwen cried, hurrying into the room.

The healer stabbed down into my wound.

I ground my tusks together, biting back the pain.

As Alwen rushed to my side, the world swam.

Everything disappeared after that.

CHAPTER 37
ALWEN

I sat by Zickar's bedside all evening, and when the sky had long since darkened, I ate quickly, brushed my teeth and washed with water in a basin, then climbed into bed with him.

"If I don't leave you, you'll be all right," I whispered against his skin. He was hot—too hot.

The healers had done what they could for him, removing the black object from his belly, giving him something to help with pain, and covering his wound with a bandage soaked in a solution that was supposed to prevent infection.

His fever raged through the night, and he thrashed, dislodging the bandage the healers had wrapped around his belly. I redid it with what they'd left behind and struggled to hold him. I did all I could to soothe him, but he kept crying out.

Dakur.

Alwen.

Shaydes.

Mother and Father.

At dawn, when my eyeballs felt stuck to my lids, someone scratched on the outer door. I got up and studied Zickar, grateful to see his chest rising and falling steadily. I hated to turn away, but when whoever it was scratched again, I hurried to the door, letting in Tenkaril, her assistant, and Sessavia.

"How is my son?" Tenkaril asked, her voice cratered with grief.

"I resecured his bandage during the night," I said. "He had a fever. He thrashed and called out."

"Have the healers seen him yet this morning?"

"Not yet."

Tenkaril lifted her hand, and her assistant leaned close to her. "Get them. Now."

"All right." He ducked out of the room.

"My son," Tenkaril sighed, using Sessavia's arm to walk into our bedroom. She sat at his side and placed her palm on his chest. "Still hot. Zickar?"

He thrashed, his eyes remaining closed.

She leaned over him, laying her thumbs on his eyelids, seeking a future I wasn't sure I wanted to know.

What would I do if I lost him? I couldn't bear the thought. We'd only been together a short time. It wouldn't be fair for the fates to steal him.

"Ah," Tenkaril said, leaning back, her hands dropping to her lap.

"What did you see?" Sessavia asked softly.

Even I eased toward her. I might not wish to know if the news was bad, but that didn't mean I wanted to hide.

"We have a long trail ahead, and it's rough and uneven," she said.

I glanced at Sessavia. "What does that mean?"

"What I said, my daughter." Tenkaril spoke gently. "I cannot say anything else about what I saw."

"Knowing doesn't necessarily mean the future will change." Funny how desperate I was to hear everything now.

"But it can." Tenkaril rose. "We will know the outcome in three days."

"Three?" I croaked, my gaze shooting to my mate who lay much too still on the bed. "What happens then?"

Tenkaril turned to me. "That's still unclear. One thing *is* clear, however." While we waited for her to speak again, she came around the bed and stopped in front of me, bracing her palms on my shoulders. "Until that time has passed, you, my daughter must take the role of caedos."

"Me?" I gulped. "I'm not trained to lead anyone."

"Few are," Tenkaril said.

"I have no idea how to do such a thing." I wrenched away from her hands, backing until I ran into the trunk of the tree.

"Do you think others know how to do this from birth? Yet they step into the role when they are called."

"I haven't been called to do this." How could she ever think I could handle such a thing? "I'm not even an orc."

"You're Zickar's mate. Since he has not yet named an heir, it's your role as his mate to lead us until he's able to do so himself."

"Then he *will* live?" I looked his way, wishing I could climb back into the bed and hold him.

"We will help you, of course." Tenkaril turned to Sessavia. "You'll be her second. She'll need guidance, naturally, but she's more than capable despite her reservations."

"I can't do this," I whispered. "Please, choose another."

"It is not me who does the choosing but the fates."

"What do you mean? You named this. The fates didn't send us a sign."

"Oh, no?" Tenkaril laughed low and soft. "Then what do you call that?" Her wizened finger lifted, pointing to my chest.

My pendant blazed like the sun.

CHAPTER 38
ZICKAR

In my dreams, I chased Taen as he raced through the forest, his long strides carrying him farther and farther away from me.

"Wait, where are you going?" I cried, but he didn't look my way. No, he had his nose to the ground as if he'd caught the perfect scent and nothing was going to keep him from following it.

What had happened to him? His brother and sister mourned his loss like I did Dakur. I was told they were often found standing on the trail leading from the clan's lands, staring in the direction I'd come from with Alwen.

Alwen. Why couldn't I wake up and see my mate, hold her?

"Zickar," she cried. "Come back to me, love."

I couldn't force my eyes open. My belly burned, and the feeling caught hold of me and dragged me back down into darkness.

I hung from a vine; my hands bound over my head with a wall to my back. A human female stood nearby, watching me with eyes like a chat's. They glanced from me to an older human male who bustled about, growling.

Periodically, he poked me, each gouge making the wound in my belly scream.

Someone helped me to the washroom and even cleansed my tusks. I groaned through it all, collapsing back onto the bed afterward and sinking into the nightmares that wouldn't release me.

I drifted from there to the edge of the forest where the humans were building a new village. More had arrived, doubling, no, quadrupling their number. They busily cut down trees.

And the trees cried out in pain.

I was yanked in yet another direction and found myself flying on a vox across the desert. Spots of lights below shifted and swayed as if the Ember Clan danced in a wild celebration. Their voices rose all the way to where my vox flew, and I tried to guide him lower so I could see what they were doing, but the vox ignored my commands just like Taen hadn't listened to my call.

"Zickar, please," Alwen cried, and I tried to lift my hand to stroke her face. I wanted to tell her everything would be all right, but I couldn't make my tongue or mouth do as I asked.

She and someone else—Sessavia?—helped me to the washroom again. I was a shaking wreck by the time I fell back on the bed, and the nightmares were eager to suck me into their dank embrace once more.

"Brother, we need you," Dakur's spirit called out to me this time. I turned to find him standing among elders I remembered from when I was young. They were dead now, just like Dakur. "Rise and do what you must. You will have help. This, I promise."

And with that, I sunk into a more comfortable sleep.

CHAPTER 39
ALWEN

The first thing I did two days after Zickar was injured was have Pulost and Finsteg stand outside our home to protect him. Then I found Sessavia dining in the central area.

"Are you any good with that blade you wear strapped to your side?" I asked her, waving off someone who tried to bring me a plate full of food, though I took a chunk of bread and bit into it.

My belly cried out, demanding nutrition. I couldn't remember when I'd last eaten.

I'd spent yesterday talking with the elders, though they didn't have much to offer. They didn't know what to do about the humans. The fates had remained silent.

They must be dueling with Zickar because he kept cursing them in his dreams.

I wanted to be with him all the time. What if he . . .

No.

I was not going to believe he could die. If I let the thought take hold, it would dig deep and fester.

"I am very good with this blade," Sessavia said softly, tapping where it remained strapped to her waist. "Do you need me to gut someone?" Her gaze slid to Ulong sitting on the opposite side of the table.

He glared her way and grunted.

"I need someone to go with me to see what the humans are up to," I said.

Her eyes widened. "Ah, now that's interesting. I hadn't considered being a guard, but the idea has merit."

"Do I need two guards like Zickar, or will you be enough?"

She grinned and rose, sliding her blade from its sheath. "I'll always be enough."

Ulong rolled his eyes.

She snarled and stormed over to stand across from him. "What? Do you think I'm not capable of doing this?"

"You're more than capable."

"Then why the snide behavior?"

"You shouldn't get too cocky."

She propped her fist on her hip and shifted it to the side. "Since I have no cock, I don't need to worry about that."

Abandoning his half-eaten meal, Ulong stood. "If you're in need of a cock . . ." A frown bloomed on his face.

Was he as surprised as those around us that he'd said this? One orc's jaw had dropped. Another held a utensil in the air, the full bite near his mouth. He didn't slide it into his gaping maw.

The third who'd been sitting beside him also stood, sending a frown Sessavia's way. "Are you all right, Ulong?" When he placed a hand on Ulong's arm, Ulong shrugged it off. He rounded the table and strode right up to Sessavia so quickly, she took a few steps backward.

"I don't . . ." He shook his head and glared at her. He reached toward her. When his fingers touched her upper arm, his pendant blazed.

Gasping, she reeled away from him, breaking contact.

He pursued her. "Mate." He said it softly. I wasn't sure if I heard anger or satisfaction in his voice.

Color rose into Sessavia's face. "I'm *not* your mate."

Ulong grinned. "Then what is the meaning of this?" He flicked her pendant that flared as brightly as his. "Shall we rut and get this over with? Then I can go to work."

She drew herself up stiffly. "You're the last male I'd ever wish to rut with."

Someone snickered. Another clapped.

I hurried over to her. "Perhaps I can find someone else to go with me to the human village."

"No!" She lowered her voice to a more normal tone. "No. I'll go."

Ulong grunted. "Then it looks like I'm traveling to the edge of the forest today as well."

ULONG AND SESSAVIA squabbled the entire time we traveled through the canopy. Other than one of them showing me how to use my pendant to call various vines, they spent all their time scowling at each other.

"You should give this mating a chance," Ulong said. I had to give him credit. He was looking at this in a practical manner.

"No chance," she snipped, her nose in the air.

How had the fates thought these two were a good match?

"You want me," Ulong growled after she'd snubbed him yet another time.

I snorted but didn't look back as I crossed a vine bridge. Bangs rang out ahead, followed by the whine of a saw, and my heart twitched with pain. They were still cutting trees. How was I going to convince them to stop?

"I'm not made for this," I grumbled, my voice lower than Ulong and Sessavia sniping at each other.

When everything went silent, I paused and frowned. I turned to find them kissing, Ulong bending Sessavia back over the side of the bridge. Her hands clutched his horns, and her moans echoed around us. She was grinding her pelvis against his.

My heart clenched like someone had grabbed it in their fist. My Zickar was unconscious. I was struggling to make this caedos thing work. And life appeared to be continuing on without us.

"Which direction?" I asked in a croaky voice.

They burst apart. Ulong gave Sessavia a tusk filled grin. She huffed and stomped toward me.

"The kiss was nothing," she said. "An aberration."

He chuckled and followed.

"Show me where to go," I said, hating to interfere in their budding romance, but I was here to do a job, and they'd insisted on coming with me to help.

Sessavia blushed. "I'm sorry. I won't get distracted again."

"You will," Ulong said with certainty. "Soon."

"Never," she vowed.

I rolled my eyes.

She strode ahead of me and called more vines, taking us forward as the sun slowly made its way down toward the horizon. Ulong followed, whistling merrily through his teeth.

Within a half an hour, we approached the edge of the forest, though I would've known a bit ago from the banging and the whine of saws.

"Let's take you far up in the canopy where *you* can see but *they* won't see you," Sessavia said, her blade in her hand and a feral look in her eyes. "No caedos will be harmed when I'm around."

"I'm here too," Ulong softly chimed in from behind us. He was much less surly than before, and more talkative. Having a mate in your life could do that, though he was going to have to work hard if he hoped to win Sessavia's heart. Funny how things could change so quickly, both for them and for me and Zickar.

I just wanted to hold him and feel his arms around me one more time. Would I be given that chance?

Sessavia called vines and a few snaked down from above us. "We must climb," she whispered, though I'd looked around and hadn't seen anyone other than us in the area.

I gaped when I looked up. "That's a vine ladder."

"You're right," she said. "It'll take us to the perfect location where you can study the situation."

I was sure I'd mostly mastered calling bridges to walk across, but this? However, everyone was counting on me to be a good leader, and while I didn't want this role—I wanted my mate healthy and able to do this himself—I was going to make him proud.

He'd wake. I was determined that it would happen. And I'd share what I saw with him. We'd come up with a plan, and things would improve for our clan.

Telling myself I was being his eyes because he couldn't be here helped.

"I'll ascend first." She grabbed onto a vine overhead and placed her foot on another, scrambling upward.

I gulped and glanced at Ulong whose gaze was focused on Sessavia's butt.

With a shake of my head, I went after her, not looking down and ignoring how flimsy the vines felt in my hands and beneath my feet.

When I reached the top, Sessavia held out her hand. I

let her tug me up onto a wide branch that struck out over the partly constructed fortress wall. Other branches loomed over it, providing decent cover.

Lying on my belly, I slithered out on the branch while Ulong and Sessavia hovered back by the trunk. Wrapping my arms around the branch, I felt secure enough to look around.

There had to be at least a hundred women busily working to construct homes as well as the outer wall. I didn't see a single male, but they could be inside the buildings. Part of the wall was finished, and they'd lined it with weapons aimed at the forest.

The ground was a long way below, but that wasn't what chilled me the most.

I slid back to the others, and we climbed down to the bridge where we'd accessed the ladder.

"I need to speak with them," I said.

"It's too dangerous," Ulong grunted.

"I doubt they'll fire at another woman." Would they, though? They hadn't hesitated with Zickar.

How was he? My heart expanded with pain, and I swallowed it back. I needed to focus on what I was doing now, not him. But what if I returned to find him gone from me already?

I had to trust the healers would help him get better, that I'd return to see him awake and looking for me.

"I have to find out why they're here," I said. "I need to see if there are men with them. And I'm going to explain fully and ask them to stop cutting the living trees."

As if they heard, the canopy overhead rustled. Though there was no wind, nearby trunks swayed. I'd never dreamed the forest could be alive with sentient trees. How could I have lived so close to the forest and hunted within it without sensing its greatness?

"Call out to them from here," Sessavia said. "Ask if they'll allow you to enter their village. Make them promise not to harm you before you do so."

How good would that promise be?

Still, I had to try. "Get me closer."

Sessavia grumbled but with vines, took me lower until I stood just inside the woods and about an orc's height above the ground.

When a woman walked past carrying a log on her shoulder, I called out. She paused and peered around.

"I'm a woman, and I'm inside the woods," I said. "Can you come closer?"

She squinted in all directions as if seeking input from someone who wasn't there before lowering the log onto the ground and cautiously walking closer to the woods, a long, thin black weapon held in her hand.

"Who is it?" she barked.

"I'm Alwen. I lived in a village near the mountains on the northern side of the forest."

The woman entered the woods and looked up, her gaze finding me. She scowled when her eyes traveled across Sessavia and Ulong, and she lifted her weapon to her mouth.

I scrambled to get in front of them, not an easy task

on a narrow vine bridge. Ulong growled and thrust me behind him, lifting his hatchet. If he threw it, he'd hit his target, but killing her wouldn't help us find a way through this tenuous situation.

"Why are you with them?" the woman asked me.

"I live with them. I'm mated to their caedos, the leader of the clan."

"Mated?" Her frown deepened. "You mean married?"

"Yes."

"Why?"

"He saved me. I was kidnapped by men—"

She spat.

Ah, so it was like that, was it?

"He rescued me, and I fell in love with him. Have you heard about the treaty the humans living in the north formed with the orcs?"

Her lips pursed. "Two poor women have to run through the woods each year while orcs hunt them, all in exchange for protection." Her spine stiffened. "If we choose to marry—*mate*—it will not be because we fear creatures in the forest." She shook her weapon. "We've already given the shaydes a few lessons in respect. Were *you* sent out during the hunt and then kidnapped?"

"I was, but I would've chosen my mate, Zickar, if given the chance." My eyes stung and again, I wondered how he was doing, if I'd get back before he . . .

No, I wasn't going to think about him dying.

"I came here to discover what you're doing," I said, my chin lifting.

Her eyebrows lifted, and she tugged her tunic down over her pants. At least she'd lowered her weapon. "We're building a village. We left our own and set out across the forest."

"Can we convince you to leave?" I asked. "You could join my village to the north."

Her body shook with her laugh. "Why would we want to do something like that? We're building a new home where *we* make our own decisions about our fate, no one else."

"You're harming the trees. They're alive. If you're going to cut any, could you please only cut those that have already died?"

"Look, you seem decent enough, so if you want to run away from the orcs, we'll welcome you with us."

"I'm not leaving them."

She huffed. "I don't have any problem with orcs in general, but if you think we're going to stop what we're doing because trees supposedly speak with you, you're wrong." She shook her head, grinning at the notion. "Go away, woman, and take your orcs with you." Pivoting, she started walking back toward where she'd left the log.

"We can't allow you to keep doing this," I called out, though I wasn't sure what we'd do to stop them.

Her low laugh echoed around us as she left the woods.

I'd failed. Why had I thought coming here and speaking with them could make a difference?

"We'll return to the clan," Sessavia said starkly. "We can discuss what must come next with the elders."

"I'm not giving up easily." I blew across my pendant, my breath catching when vines snaked out at my command, connecting with the ones I stood on and leading down to the forest floor. Truly, I didn't know the specific command to ask this from the vines; they'd responded solely due to luck.

I needed this luck, however, and I was going to claim it.

Over their protests, I descended to the ground and walked through the woods to the right, making my way to where a few women worked on a gate. This time, when I called out, three of them approached me, scanning the woods. They also held black weapons like the first, and the thought of one of them lifting it and shooting Zickar made me want to grab my blade and slice through them all.

I bit back the urge.

"Hide," I hissed to Sessavia and Ulong, unable to bear the thought of them getting hurt.

They remained nearby, flanking me.

The women stopped on the edge of the forest, peering in my direction, though I wasn't sure they could see me. "Who is it?"

"It sounded like a woman to me," one said.

"Might've been one of those giant lizards playing tricks with our minds," another said.

"They only come out at night. And I heard a woman."

She lifted her voice. "Hey! Identify yourself and come out of the woods slowly."

"Can I do so safely?"

"I suppose so."

I pulled my blade and walked out to meet them.

"It *is* a woman," a tall woman about my age said, looking me up and down. "What are you doing out here? Don't you know there are predators and orcs around?"

"I'm here representing the Matis Clan."

A woman with black hair and rich brown skin glanced at the others in confusion. "Who are they?"

"They're the orcs who live in this area," I said.

"Orcs. You're here to represent *orcs*?" The tall woman rubbed her ear. "I couldn't have heard you right."

I explained everything again.

They started laughing.

"Go back to your orcs," the dark-haired woman finally said. "Leave us alone."

"You have to stop," I shouted.

The tall woman grabbed my upper arm. Ulong growled in the woods behind me.

The woman frowned, squinting in that direction. "Look. It's been nice speaking with you, but we've got work to do."

They turned and walked back to the gate.

"I mean it," I called out, feeling helpless. Useless. Utterly frustrated.

One of the women lifted her weapon, and I backed into the woods. "Go away. Leave us alone."

I returned to my friends who gaped toward the fortress in horror.

"Let's return to our village," I said softly. "As you said, we need to speak with the elders about this latest development."

But when we returned, the elders were busy.

The Flazants had arrived to collect Dillu and the girls.

CHAPTER 40

ZICKAR

I clawed my way out of my nightmares and bolted upright in my bed.

"Zickar," Alwen cried. She rose from where she lay beside me and put her arms around me. "Zickar. Please come back to me."

I turned and cupped her face. "I'm here for you, mate." Always. This was the only place I wanted to be.

"You're awake. You're you."

My low chuckle rang out, but the movement made my abdomen ache. "What happened? I remember something piercing my belly. A human weapon. It burned when it hit. Pulost and Finsteg . . ."

Alwen explained.

"You've been acting as caedos?" Funny how I focused on that detail among all the others.

"I've done what I could for three days. I went to the

humans and asked them to stop cutting the living trees, but they laughed at me."

I eased her away from me and studied her body. She wore a light garment for sleeping. "You're not wounded?"

"They only threatened me. They didn't fire. I've never seen a weapon like that before. When they place it against their mouths, they're able to shoot something through it. It's not a bow and arrow. It's unlike a spear."

"Whatever it is, we need to be wary. It could cause our clan great harm."

"We need to do something about them," she said fiercely. "Make them leave."

"We'll speak with the elders."

"We?"

"I told you I would be proud to have you standing by my side, and now you are."

"Tenkaril announced the fates wanted me to lead while you were sick." Her face scrunched up. "I can't imagine why."

"You're smart. Brave. That's why."

"I have so much left to learn. The women in the new village laughed at me. They didn't take me seriously when they should. Our clan is strong. There are more of us than them. And only *we* can hold back the shaydes and ashenclaws."

"You're so strong." I tipped up her chin. "Incredibly beautiful."

She pressed herself against me. "I was worried about

you. You were hurt, and you wouldn't wake. The healers didn't know what to do."

"I'm fine. Much better. I had such odd dreams." I frowned, trying to remember, before nudging the thoughts aside. My mate was here with me, and they were just misty images my mind had created. She was all I wanted to focus on now.

A glance showed me it was night.

"Help me?" I asked, waving to the washroom and hating that I felt as if I couldn't travel the distance by myself.

She slid off the bed and held out her hand, tugging me close when I stood. At least my legs still worked. My cock too.

"Feeling better, I see," she said, shooting a smile up at me. "Let's get you to the washroom, and then back to bed where you can continue to rest."

My cock had more than rest in mind.

"I hate that I can barely move on my own," I grumbled as she supported me into the smaller, attached room.

I took care of my needs, then washed and cleansed my tusks and teeth.

When she helped me back to bed, I collapsed on my back. Only my cock still had any strength, the damn thing stabbing toward the ceiling.

"My mate has needs," she said in a sultry voice, trailing her fingertip down my length. "You're weak, but I believe I can help you in this as well."

When had she turned into a seductress? I welcomed this, however. Welcomed her in any way, shape, or form.

"Mate," I growled.

She climbed up onto me and spread her legs around my hips, my cock jutting up between us.

She kissed me, and I lost track of everything but her. With a moan, she clutched my shoulders and rocked against my length.

There were so many ways I wanted to love her, be with her. Would a lifetime be enough to enjoy them all?

At least my hands still worked. I found her clit and stroked it, sliding one finger deep inside her. She rode my finger, her head tipping back, and there wasn't anyone prettier, more arousing than my pretty maiden.

My heart flailed against my ribs as she lifted and let herself drop back down. I was going to explode, and I wasn't even inside her yet.

"Take me, love," I growled. "I'm yours for this lifetime and beyond."

Her gaze locked on mine, and she nudged my fingers away. Taking my cock in her hand, she lifted up, centered it at her opening, and sunk down on top of me. She took everything I had so sweetly.

"Tight," I groaned, nearly exploding already.

"Keep that thought," she said with a smile. "Don't let go yet." As my spur latched onto her clit, she started moving, picking herself up and dropping down hard, impaling my length inside her wet passage.

I moved up to meet her, driving myself slowly before

increasing my pace based on her sighs and moans and how fast she lifted her body and dropped. Knowing I could give this woman what she needed was the joy I'd sought all my life.

Her head tipped back and there was no one more gorgeous than my mate finding her satisfaction.

The creases on her face and her high-pitched moans told me all I needed to know. I took joy in life, in this moment. There couldn't be anything better than this.

"Yes," she shouted as her body started to fall apart. "Love you, Zickar. My mate."

I couldn't wait to come inside her, to feel her body quivering around mine.

And when she gave into her bliss, I joined her, pushing up against her final thrust.

CHAPTER 41
ALWEN

We washed in the bathing chamber in the big tub together.

Then we went to the central dining area. Zickar's footsteps were shaky, but he was able to carry himself. Once he'd eaten and rested some more, I was confident he'd return to his old self. The cheers that greeted him at the entrance to the dining area warmed me through. I didn't take it personally that they were grateful he lived and would resume his duties. I'd done what I could, but they adored him as they should.

Tenkaril paused at our table as she was leaving, scanning us both as if she could see without touching. "I'm grateful you're well, my son."

"I feel almost myself." He might say this, but I could see how his hand trembled as he held his eating implement. It was going to take time for him to fully regain his strength.

"Your mate has done well." She nodded to me. "She gave us the information we need to handle this human problem."

I wasn't sure what information I'd delivered other than that there were a lot more humans in the new village than before, there didn't appear to be any men, and that they all had long black sticks they used to shoot tiny bits of metal on a whim.

All this, I'd shared with Zickar while we bathed.

"Once you've finished eating," Tenkaril said. "We must meet with the elders. The Flazant leader came with a contingent, and she may have some input."

I'd also told Zickar they'd come to collect our friends.

Zickar nodded slowly, chewing the last of his bread. "I'd love to hear her thoughts."

"I'll see you shortly, then," she said. Her smile took in me as well. "*Both* of our caedos." With that, she took her assistant's arm, and they left the dining room.

"I'm not really a caedos," I said, leaning into Zickar's side. "That's your position."

"If my mother feels you are, then it's true."

"I'll happily join you and the elders during the discussion, but I'm not sure what I'll have to say that will make a difference."

"You don't give yourself enough credit, mate."

Perhaps.

We left and made our way across a series of trees using vines I called with my pendant. I didn't shake or stop once while standing on the platforms, and the height didn't seem to bother me as much as it had before.

Zickar grinned. "Look at you. You're clan now, mate."

"I'm trying to fit in." But it was more than that. I wanted to learn everything I could about my new people. I wasn't an orc, and no one seemed to care about that, but in my heart, I wanted to feel as if I belonged.

Since the Flazants would join us and their stony bodies were much larger than ours, we took a teegar down to the ground.

Two shaydes met with us as we walked along a path toward the big open meadow where we'd talk about what we could do next.

One of the shaydes licked Zickar's face while the other sniffed me. I held perfectly still, afraid the beast would eat me, but it soon gave me what almost looked like a grin and nuzzled my hand.

"They enjoy having their cheeks stroked," Zickar said, demonstrating with the other shayde.

I tentatively touched the one near me, and it purred.

Another test from my clan, and it appeared I'd passed this one as well.

An older orc male appeared on the path with a pouch strapped to his back.

He nodded to Zickar, his gaze scanning me, though in a polite way. "I'm ready to leave. This won't take long."

"I hope not." Zickar strode over to him and braced the other male's upper arms. "Thank you. Travel carefully and return to us soon."

"I will." He sent me a smile before he leaped onto one of the shaydes. At his urging, it rushed down the path, the other shayde running behind the first.

"Where is he going?" I asked.

"Rusket has a small errand to complete for me. It's nothing."

"All right."

Holding hands, we walked farther, finally striding out into a meadow. About twenty of our fellow clan joined us, though most remained along the edge of the woods.

The sun shone down, and a light breeze stirred my hair. There couldn't be a lovelier day, and I wished the humans had never come to our part of the forest. There were other places where they could build their village. Why harm our trees to live in this area?

Funny how I saw their ugly wooden homes as ruining the forest. But I swore I could feel the pain experienced by the trees. It hadn't taken me long to see how the Matis Clan respected the living world around them. They took what they needed to survive but they gave back in equal measure, planting new trees to replace the old and caring for the eldest among the forest. Four orcs had been assigned this duty, and during mealtime, I'd overheard them speaking about how to remove infestations in bark and how to coax the effervast trees to bloom. When they did, the area was filled with the beautiful fragrance, but even more, the blossoms could be eaten.

Soon, our three elders strolled into the meadow and sat on the ground in the center. The earth shook as the Flazants approached, and I wasn't the only one who gulped. When they appeared, ducking their heads through gaps in the vegetation, their rocky bodies following. Even I had to suppress an urge to leap to my feet to keep from being trampled.

They had to be twice as large as Dillu.

The girls skipped into the open area along with them, their faces wreathed with smiles. Dillu followed holding his club, ducking his head in my direction when he saw me.

They settled on the ground, one of them nodding my way, though I hadn't yet met him. They'd arrived last night, and instead of going to them, I'd returned to my home to watch over Zickar.

"Thank you all for gathering with us to talk about this problem," Tenkaril said. She shared what had happened already with the Flazants.

Pirrah, the Flazant leader, looked toward Zickar. "You have healed?"

Zickar shifted, wincing, though I doubted anyone else noticed. "Yes, I'm well."

"And you were unharmed?" Pirrah directed this to me, her gaze sliding to Sessavia and Ulong standing with the others. They stood side by side, but still separate enough that I suspected they hadn't decided what to make of their new mate bond.

Ulong's pendant suddenly blazed, as did Sessavia's, and they looked at each other with bewilderment.

"I'm well also," I said.

"These weapons," Pirrah said. "They pierce the flesh, but does anyone know if they can penetrate Flazant skin?" She ran her hand down her arm, and the sound of two rocks rubbing together rang out.

"No," Tenkaril said. "We, of course, would never test anything like that on the young."

"Dillu says happy to see what black sticks do," Trillie said, nudging her brother's side. He nodded.

"If testing is to be done," Pirrah said sternly. "One of the adults will do so." She turned back to us.

"Diplomacy hasn't worked," Tenkaril said. "They attacked Zickar before he could speak, and while they allowed Alwen to talk with them, they laughed at her and told her they had no intention of stopping what they are doing."

"They're killing our precious trees," someone shouted from the gathering crowd. "We should kill them instead!"

"Enough," Tenkaril said, though softly.

Silence descended. She didn't need to bellow to make her point.

"We will not indiscriminately attack another species," she said. "Despite them attacking us. As much as I'd love to seek revenge for them nearly killing my son, we haven't lived in harmony with the forest all this time only to create discord with a species who might be coaxed into doing the same."

"Do we believe they fully understand what they're doing?" I asked. It might be bold of me to speak during their meeting, but she said I should be here. Why else but to give input? "Despite my telling them otherwise, a tree is a tree to them. They didn't seem to care that chopping down live trees was the same as killing one of us or themselves."

"*We* could speak with them," Pirrah said. "And determine if their black sticks are something for the Flazants to be worried about." She lifted her arm, and one of the Flazants bent close. "Go explain to these humans exactly what they're doing. In case there's been a mistake, make sure they understand that cutting down living trees is harming the forest. More so, that it's forbidden. If you can, see if the black sticks cause us harm, though don't endanger yourself to do so. Perhaps ask?"

"All right." The Flazant bowed and stomped across the meadow, disappearing into the woods.

"This won't take long," Pirrah said. "Wambak will return shortly."

"Walking will take quite some time," Zickar said.

Pirrah smiled. "Then it's good that he won't be walking, isn't it?"

Soon, the cry of a very large creature rang out, followed by the rustle of enormous wings.

"A vox?" I asked Zickar softly, peering up at the sky.

He shrugged. "The ones I've seen aren't large enough to carry a Flazant."

"You're correct, Caedos Zickar," Pirrah said.

"While we wait, I'm seeking other ideas," Tenkaril said. "Elders? Anyone?"

"Sabotage," Pulost said. "If we burn their new homes, they'll flee."

"And what if they don't flee?" Zickar asked. "What if they come here and burn *our* homes in retaliation?"

"We can live below the ground," he said, though in a reasonable enough tone. I got the idea he was upset with himself that Zickar had been injured, that he felt responsible in some way. He partly was because he'd been sent with Zickar as a guard. But Zickar had taken the initiative to walk out toward the humans on his own. Pulost wasn't responsible for that.

"Those who live below ground adore that life," Zickar said. "But what if the humans learn how to use the teegars and follow us?"

"We'll go deeper," Pulost said. Even I could see the weakness in his argument.

Zickar shook his head. "How deep will we need to go to keep them from us?"

Pulost's face darkened. "You're correct. I didn't think this through."

"All ideas are welcome," Zickar said. "Yours has merit."

Pulost nodded.

"I have an idea," I said in the silence that followed.

"Can you do something about those pendants?" Finsteg asked Ulong, shielding his eyes from their stars that continued to blaze.

"I'd like to, but Sessavia doesn't think she needs a mate," Ulong said in disgust. "I'm a good male. Strong." He demonstrated by making a muscle in his upper arm, and it was impressive. Working with metal had added bulk to his already large orc frame.

"It takes more than strength to win a mate," Sessavia said carefully.

"The fates chose," Tenkaril said as if that was all anyone needed to know who they should marry. "Go mate and be done with it."

Sessavia drew herself up. "His kiss is appealing, but I don't believe he'll make me the best mate."

"So, you like my kiss?" Ulong asked with a grin. "Why not try the rest of me before you decide?"

"You two," Tenkaril chided. "Cover your pendants." She looked Sessavia's way. "I would never suggest you force this, but if you enjoy his kiss, you may enjoy more."

Sessavia looked Ulong up and down. "I'll give you one night."

"That'll be enough." Ulong's grin widened as he placed his palm over his pendant.

"Now that we have that settled, you had something you wished to say, Caedos Alwen?" Tenkaril asked, her head tilting. She had that look in her eyes I'd only noticed when she "saw". She'd touched me. Had she told me everything she'd seen? I suspected not.

"Perhaps we should look at this from a different direction. What do they need?" I asked. "If we can figure that out, we can form a truce."

"I'd prefer to find a way to work with them than drive them away," Tenkaril said.

"Do they need us to show them the difference between live and dead wood?" someone suggested.

"How about protection from the shaydes?" another called out. "That worked with Alwen's village."

"Which is where my mind is going," I said.

Tenkaril nodded, a smile twitching across her lips. That sly elder. She *had* seen this coming.

Someone grunted. "We need to bury all their weapons, and then they'll need us."

"Actually . . ." I said. "I know just what they may need most."

Eyes widened and a hush descended over the meadow.

"What if we offer them orc mates?" I asked.

CHAPTER 42

ZICKAR

See? My mate was clever. No wonder I adored her above all others.

"This has merit," Pulost said. "But how will we talk about such a thing if they shoot their metal weapons at us?"

"It's worth a try, don't you think?" Alwen said. "I can go back and ask them. If they agree, we'll infiltrate them with orc mates. Then we can educate them about what they're doing with the trees. Wouldn't some of you like to meet women who could make your pendants blaze?"

A few heads nodded.

Tenkaril chuckled. "Our co-caedos is very wise."

"I think they might consider this," someone said from the edge of the meadow. Wambak, the Flazant who'd left to speak with the women had returned, his arms loaded with their long black weapons. "They didn't fire upon me initially." His low, rumbling laugh rang out, a grating sound that still somehow came out melodic. "I talked to them about the trees, how they are alive, how they feel pain."

"What did they say?" Alwen asked, leaning forward.

"Like with you, they laughed." He shook his head. "They don't seem to believe me. Perhaps they can't hear the tree's voices in the rustle of their leaves, in the wind drifting across their branches?"

"How did you end up with their weapons, and can I look at them?" Pirrah held out her hand.

He dropped them onto the ground with a clatter and gave her one.

She tipped it this way and that, looking at it from all angles while the rest of us poked at the rest of the pile.

"They don't appear to act on their own," she finally said. "I don't believe they're alive."

Tenkaril touched one and shook her head. "They're dead things. Deadly as well. They're constructed of a material similar to what orcs use to line the outer walls of their homes in the kingdom near the sea."

"How do they send tiny bits of metal into flesh?" I asked, peering through the end of one, noting it was hollow.

"They did this." Wambak lifted one and placed a pebble in one end. He held it to his mouth. "Stand back. Even a small rock might hurt if it hits you." He fumbled with the other end before growling with irritation. "My fingers are too large." He waved for Alwen to come closer. "Help me, would you, caedos?"

She gingerly took the weapon from him and placed it against her mouth.

"Suck in a deep breath and blow through it hard."

Alwen looked my way, her eyes wide, but did as he instructed. When she blew through the device, the pebble was flung against the ground near a tree. Pulost and Finsteg went over and bent down in that area.

"It embedded itself into the soil," Pulost said with wonder.

Finsteg's gaze narrowed on the pile of metal weapons. "I'm going to practice with this until I can aim it. Then I'll teach everyone who wishes to learn. If they don't cooperate, we can use their own weapons against them."

"You don't appear wounded," I told Wambak, looking him over.

"Their metal bits bounce off Flazants." He grinned and puffed out his chest. "So as they tried to make their weapons wound me, I went around and collected them."

"Do they have others?" Tenkaril asked.

"I don't believe so," he said. "Though I didn't search their dwellings." He shrugged. "I wouldn't fit inside them if I tried."

"If they do, I doubt they have many," Alwen said. She sent a smile my way. "Now that it appears we've taken away their advantage, we can approach them and make them listen."

"And if they don't?"

She looked around. "Who here would like to see if any of them are your mates?"

"I would," someone called out.

One of our females snorted. "I'd have to look them over first, but I'm not opposed to the idea."

Others nodded, and soon, more had gathered, stating they'd be willing to chance the black sticks if that meant they might find a mate.

"It seems we have a solution," I said. "Now we just need to convince the humans that they have a problem."

CHAPTER 43
ALWEN

The next morning, we met at one of the largest meadows before departing to make our offer to the women.

A loud whoosh rang out, and an enormous bird landed in the center of the open area, casting its beady eyes my and Zickar's way.

"They only eat bugs," Wambak said when I reeled back from the creature. He ran his fingertips through its long feathers. "You're safe, tiny human."

I leaned into Zickar's embrace, his arms enfolding me and keeping me safe. "They're gorgeous." I took in their pale green wings flecked with lavender and their bright red beaks.

Wambak leaped up onto the bird's back, and it peered back at him, seemingly unconcerned about his stony weight. At his command, it took flight, and other birds like the first landed, one for each Flazant.

"Want to go," Trillie said, Brillie and Villadeer nodding. Even Dillu looked sad that he wasn't part of this operation.

"When you're older, you'll go on your own adventure," Tenkaril said sagely. "I've seen this."

"Oh, good," Villadeer said. "Thought entire life living with Flazants." She fingered her new pendant. "Learn call wind. Wind!" Lifting her pendant, she blew across it and a breeze stirred the canopy. "See?"

"Amazing," I said.

"Your clan is wonderful. Be happy that you have a chance to go home," Tenkaril said, patting Villadeer's shoulder. The Flazant children were so large, they even towered over most of the orcs.

Sessavia joined us with a dreamy look in her eyes. I noted her pendant wasn't blazing, but Ulong wasn't around yet.

"Are you . . . all right?" I asked, walking over to her.

She huffed. "As you may know, last night I gave Ulong a chance."

I lifted my eyebrows, my lips twitching with humor. "And?"

She winked. "I might give him another chance tonight."

As I'd thought earlier. Their romance was going to be a lot of fun to watch.

"Other than our two caedos, eight orcs will travel with us to the humans," Tenkaril said, speaking to the gathering crowd of orcs who'd come to see us off. "Unmated males and females only, please."

Pulost eased his way through the group. "I'd like to go." He looked Zickar's way for permission.

My mate nodded. "I believe you'll be an asset to our clan."

"May I as well?" Finsteg asked, and he was also given permission.

The orc female who'd expressed interest the day before also stepped forward. "If I might? I'm curious to see if all females are as attractive as our caedos."

I shot her a grin. "And if they are?"

Her smile rose to match mine. "Then I may select one."

"Your pendant and the fates do the selecting," Tenkaril said with a snort. "Please remember this."

The orc female dipped her head Tenkaril's way.

"If you'll allow me?" Tenkaril asked Zickar. "I'd like to choose the others." At his wave, she walked among those gathered, touching one and then another.

Soon, the rest of the Flazants had taken flight and eight orcs had joined us in the center of the meadow.

"Go swiftly, my son," Tenkaril said, curling her fingertip his way so she could *see* him.

He bent forward and she placed her thumbs on his closed eyelids.

"Yes," she said, backing away.

"Will our plan work?" I asked.

"*Your* plan, my daughter. You suggested this. As for

whether it will work, it has a chance, and just like with Ulong and Sessavia," she cast a heavy look Sessavia's way, "where there's a chance, there's a potential future one may never dream of."

"He's good, but I'm not yet sure he's *that* good," Sessavia said with a low laugh.

"I heard that," Ulong said, striding into the meadow. He grinned at Sessavia. "I seem to remember one particular orc female shrieking out her pleasure more than once last night."

She blushed.

"I won't be coming with you," Tenkaril told me and Zickar. "This is for eight orcs and you two to settle. But I have hope, and when that resides in my heart, anything is possible."

We took the bagged supplies one of the orcs had gathered for us and left, traveling together across vine bridges to the western edge of the forest.

Soon, we joined the Flazants on the ground, standing just inside the woods.

"They've made a lot of progress," I whispered, pointing to the finished fortress wall. "The shaydes and ashenclaws won't get past that."

"Yet they're trapped inside a small area," Wambak said, stomping his way over to join us. They'd landed their birds in the canopy and leaped to the ground, somehow landing silently so as not to draw the humans' attention. "We noted how small their area is as we flew overhead."

"They may be more eager to negotiate, then," I said.

"We go together," Zickar said. "Watch for black sticks. I'm confident Wambak took them all, but they could've had some hidden."

We called out before we left the woods to alert them we were coming. While it would be nice to stomp forward, lay out our terms, and demand they take them, we wanted peace, not endless battle.

The dark-haired woman with tight curly hair and brown skin cracked open the front gate of their fortress, poking her head out. "You're back? Have you come to continue the silly stories about living trees?"

A branch dropped from overhead, landing so close to the gate, it scraped across the surface. She gasped, peering upward.

"That didn't happen," she said.

"Would you like another demonstration?" Zickar asked, lifting his pendant. "I can speak to the trees. While they won't uproot and attack you, they have other ways of making their presence known."

"Do it. I don't believe you."

He blew softly across his pendant and at least a thousand twigs flew from the forest, impaling themselves in the gate's surface.

The woman gaped at the fluttering twigs, paling. "All right." She frowned at the forest. "I see you!"

"It's a start," Zickar told me.

The woman stepped out beyond the gate with three others following.

"I'm the leader of this village. Why have you come here?" Her gaze slid down Zickar's body, though not in a sexual way. "Aren't you the one I shot?"

Zickar lifted one side of his unibrow. "I've recovered."

"I . . . didn't mean to fire on you like that. You startled me!"

The other humans murmured agreement.

"We've come here to make you a generous offer," I said, striding forward. "Would you be willing to let us inside to discuss it?"

"Orcs and . . . well, whatever the stone people are? No, I can't let you inside. I'm sorry, but it's just not done. Surely you understand."

I dipped my head forward, saying nothing.

"I'm Mavileen, by the way," she said. "I'm the duly elected mayor of this fine village."

"It's nice to meet you," I said, though I wasn't sure I truly meant it.

"The Flazants are peaceful people," Zickar pointed out, waving to them standing near the edge of the woods.

Mavileen grunted. "That's what everyone says." She removed her hand from the blade strapped to her side. The other women remained alert with spears and long blades in their hands. So far, I hadn't seen any black metal devices. "What's your offer?" Her eyebrows lifted as she looked us over.

Behind me, Pulost gasped and uttered a guttural cry. I peered over my shoulder, only to find his pendant blazing. He strode past us and right up to the Mavileen. "I, Pulost, member of the Brialon faction of the Matis Clan, claim you as my mate."

Mavileen's eyebrows rose even higher as she looked him up and down. "I'm not sure I even want to know what that means, but if you think saying something fancy does much for me, you need to take your thoughts in a different direction."

"You're my mate," he said. "Come, and I'll ensure you have endless satisfaction."

She huffed. "I assume you mean sexually."

"Of course." He almost sounded insulted that she wasn't gushing all over him.

"I'm not interested in getting married at this time, though I'll mention that you're attractive in your own, orcish way."

"You're my mate," he growled, truly sounding insulted now.

"Just because you've declared something doesn't mean it's true," she said shortly. She strode around him and up to me. "What are you offering?"

"Well, we're offering mates," I said with a laugh. If the situation wasn't a bit frightening, it could be considered comical. Actually, it *was* comical. "Pulost's clan pendant will only blaze when the fates choose his true mate for him. That's you."

"Not today. Although, orcs are something else, aren't they?" She shook her head. "Imagine thinking they can stride up to someone, make a declaration like that, and expect a woman to swoon." She glared at Pulost. "I'm not swooning."

"You will." He fed her a grin. "Because I'm good. Very good."

She drew herself up stiffly. "I left the protection of our fortress to discuss a deal, not contemplate sex with an orc." Her gaze dropped to his loincloth where his big cock was shifting. "Do you . . . wear a device underneath your clothing?"

"What you see, mate, is all me," Pulost said. "With this, I'll give you great satisfaction."

"Males sure are cocky about what's between their legs, aren't they?" she asked me.

This conversation was getting away from me. "Here's what we propose. Stop cutting living trees and use only those that have died from disease or weather. In exchange, we'll not only allow you to remain here, but we'll also introduce any woman interested in mating to some very fine orcs like Pulost. Eight have come with us today as a show of good faith. It's clear we have something to offer since Pulost has already started to bond with you."

"So Pulost thinks," she said with a low chuckle. "I'm not yet in agreement."

"You will be," he said, his smile widening. "Shall I give you a sample of what I have to offer?"

I laid my hand on his arm. "Later. Please."

He frowned down at me, his face clearing and color darkening his cheeks. "I'm sorry. You're correct, Caedos.

We must wait until our agreement is settled. *Then*, I will show her."

"What does caedos mean?" Mavileen asked.

"My mate," I linked my arm through Zickar's, "and I share the leadership of our clan. Caedos means leader."

"A human woman leads orcs? I like this. This is why we left our home far to the west of here. Males kept trying to tell us what to do. They refused to allow us much say in what we did with our lives." Her head tilted, and she studied the entire group. "What do the stone people—Flazants—have to do with all this?"

"They're our friends."

"Your friends took all our weapons."

"You use them, you lose them."

Zickar chuckled and spoke low by my ear. "And you thought you wouldn't be good at this?"

"Do you agree to our offer?" I asked Mavileen.

Two of the women started looking over the eligible males, and one even strode around one. His pendant blazed, and he took her hand and kissed it.

She blushed and shot Mavileen a pleading look. "Maybe we should consider their offer."

Mavileen grumbled, but she couldn't take her eyes off Pulost. "All right. We'll do it. We won't cut live trees, and your clan will . . . provide mates. *If* we want them. Remember, however, we want independence, not to trade subjugation from human males for that of orcs. If any of us don't want to be with an orc, we won't allow that person to be forced."

"We can be very accommodating," Pulost said. "*Very*."

"You're handsome, but not *that* handsome," she quipped. From the way she kept checking out his cock, I had a feeling it wouldn't be long before she allowed him to give her a sample of what he had to offer.

"I can be," he said. "Try me."

I held out my hand. "Do we have a deal?"

Mavileen gave it a shake. "Yes, we have a deal."

CHAPTER 44
ZICKAR

We took the slow route back to the clan, and if Alwen and I happened to slip away from the others—Alwen winking at Sessavia to assure her everything was all right—then so be it.

I'd started to recover from the wound delivered by the humans, we'd formed a truce that would protect our trees, and Alwen and I were in love.

I wanted to take some time away from the others to show her how much she meant to me.

"The Flazants will be leaving soon," she said when we stopped in a mossy area I thought would be perfect to lounge in for a bit.

"If I know my mother, she'll host a goodbye party for them."

"Can you believe what we just did?" She lifted her arms and spun around in the open area, laughing. "We made a truce with another village! Our people will find mates, and the trees are safe once more."

"Did you see the way Mavileen was looking at Pulost?"

"And another match was made almost instantly. As for Mavileen, I doubt she'll hold out for long. It looks like Pulost will end up *mated* with a leader."

"That should make him happy in many ways. Funny how the fates know how to bring two people together."

"They picked my perfect match when they sent me to you."

"Zickar," she sighed, tracing her fingertip down my chest and across my abs—making me laugh because it tickled—then along my cock that was already eager. "Love me."

"I do. I always will." I tugged her into my arms. "I want to prove that we're alive. I need your touch more than anything."

"You make my world right, Zickar." She sent me a shy smile that made my heart expand to three times its size. I couldn't adore this woman any more than I did right now.

I gave her a quick kiss. Or one that was supposed to be quick but turned into longer and brought on considerable moaning on both our parts.

Then I carefully removed her clothing, pausing to kiss each of her limbs on the way. Once I'd removed my loincloth, we dropped to the ground.

And as we came together, we celebrated our mating, our love, and the joy we'd found with each other.

CHAPTER 45
EPILOGUE
ALWEN

The next morning, after eating fish we caught in the river and sleeping in a tree, though we spent more time loving each other than sleeping, we returned to the clan village, arriving as the Flazants were getting ready to depart.

Tenkaril sent us a smile when we joined everyone in the large meadow. "There you are. I was just telling Wambak that I hope they visit again. I'd also love to travel to where they live one day, though I'd prefer to ride a shayde over flying on one of their giant birds. One might peck me!"

Two of the Flazants were busy grooming the birds. One turned its head to scratch beneath one of its enormous wings with its beak. As if sensing my attention, it paused and looked my way. I swore it winked.

I gulped, and Zickar's arms went around me. "Interesting creatures, aren't they, pretty maiden?"

"Very."

Wambak left the woods and strode over to stand with us. "Would you like to meet the one who graciously allows me to ride on her back?"

When he held out his hand, I took it.

"I'd also love to learn more about your pets," Zickar said, coming with us.

"They're not pets," Wambak said, though kindly. "No more than your shaydes."

"Actually, shaydes are pets, right?" I asked Zickar with a frown.

"Sometimes."

A shiver shot through me. I'd interacted with the two enough that I was no longer afraid of them. Did I have to worry again about turning my back?

"They might lick you," Zickar said, watching my face. A laugh burst from him, and he tugged me close, kissing my temple and whispering for my ears alone. "As will I."

"You." Shaking my head, I stepped around him and approached the bird Wambak had started grooming with a brush the size of my head.

Dillu and the girls walked closer to the bird with us, the girls chattering about all the things they were going to do once they got home.

"We play games Alwen teach us," Villadeer said. "Make friends jealous." She lifted her pendant. "And I create wind!"

I had a feeling it was going to be quite windy in their village.

"We share games with friends," Brillie said with a big smile.

Trillie shrugged. "Only if they nice."

"I'm going to miss you, girls," I said, and we hugged as one. When we pulled apart, it was all I could do not to cry.

"Come closer," Wambak said. "You can brush her if you'd like." He held the brush out to me as I joined him. When I ran it along the creature's front leg, it shook its head and squawked.

My laugh burst out, and it peered at me again. This time I knew it purposefully winked.

Many assumed creatures didn't understand the ways of orcs and humans. Most of them also believed trees couldn't tell anyone when they were in pain. Those who refused to truly "see" the world around them lived a bleaker life than they could ever know. Our world was rich and full of wonder. Without savoring each part of it, we were truly lost.

Zickar lifted a second brush and started grooming the bird beside me.

Tenkaril came over to join us. "Are you sure you can't stay a bit longer? There's no rush for you to return to your home, is there?"

"Oh, but there is," Wambak said. "There's a woman I've been watching. I'm going to ask her to be my mate."

"Will she accept you?" I asked, hoping she would. He was a sweet male and he deserved someone who'd love him.

"She'd better." Turning, he gave me a smile. "What do you think, Alwen? Will a human be willing to mate with a Flazant?"

"I bet she will." I patted his arm, hoping things went well for him.

Stomps rang out in the woods behind us, and I turned.

The shaydes burst into the meadow, each loaded with people.

My knees shook, and I nearly collapsed on the ground as the male who'd ridden away with the shaydes the day before helped my beloved mother, my sisters, and my brother slide off the creature's backs.

"Well, can you believe that?" Zickar said, wrapping his arm around my back and squeezing me. "Looks like Rusket has found a few humans wandering around in the forest and brought them to us."

My eyes stung with tears as I looked up at him. "Thank you. Thank you."

He gave me a kiss then urged me in their direction.

"Alwen?" my mother cried, rushing toward me with her arms spread wide.

I met her halfway across the meadow, and we sobbed, hugging each other.

"An orc came to the village," she finally said, wiping the tears off her face. "He said he was sent by a friend to bring us to you if we so wished. He made many promises, and I took his word for it, but . . ."

"Is it true that we're welcome here?" Nayleen asked. "That they welcome expert seamstresses?"

"We do," Zickar said joining us.

"This is my mate, Zickar," I said proudly, introducing him to my sisters, brother, and my mother.

He kissed her cheek. "All are welcome in the Matis Clan."

Mother's eyes widened as she looked Zickar up and down. "You've found love, Alwen?" I knew exactly what she meant. After all, she'd helped me bury my past.

"I have." I leaned into Zickar's side. "Zickar is sweet, loving, and I couldn't be happier."

Her posture loosened. "I'm so happy to hear that." She stumbled forward and hugged Zickar. "If it's all right with you, I'll call you son."

"Please do."

"We'll settle you in a lovely home," I said. "And take you to Ulong for pendants. You'll need them to travel through the canopy, and we'll teach you how to use them."

My brother, Bredar, gaped up at the canopy. "We can travel through the treetops?"

"It's amazing."

"You don't like heights," my youngest sister, Creea said.

"I do now."

"If you'll be so kind as to come with me," Rusket said, his gaze lingering for a long time on my mother.

She peeked at him through her lashes, and I

wondered if her new pendant would soon flash for an orc. Only time would tell.

"Where will you take us, Rusket?" she asked him with a sweet smile.

"First, to your new home. Then, if you'd like, we could dine together in the central eating area."

She placed her hand on his forearm and blinked up at him. "I'd like that very much." Her gaze fell on me. "We'll see you soon, Alwen?"

"Very soon. Once we've said goodbye to our friends, I'll come find you."

Rusket led them from the meadow and not long later, my brother's shout of joy rang out, telling me he'd just taken his first ride on a teegar.

"You, mate, are amazing," I said, hugging Zickar.

"I only want you happy, love."

"I am."

We kissed, and when we parted, we walked back to the Flazants who were getting ready to leave.

They took off one by one until only Wambak, mounted on his large bird, remained.

"As for that small task you gave me, Tenkaril," he said. "I promise I'll send word the moment I hear something."

"Thank you," she said from partway across the meadow.

I still couldn't believe my family was here. I'd show them the underground homes. We'd swim in the river.

I'd take my brother hunting again. And my sisters . . . They were going to be so happy living here.

I owed it all to my love, my Zickar.

As if he knew my thoughts, his arm went around me, holding me close. He kissed the top of my head, and there was no feeling better than the love he showed me every moment of my life.

"What do you need, Mother?" Zickar asked.

She came over to stand on my other side, also giving me a quick hug. "Wambak has promised to send someone to ask a few questions of the Ember Clan."

"Oh?" Zickar shot me a confused look, and I shrugged, having no more idea what she meant than him.

"Dakur," Tenkaril said. She pivoted and took her assistant's arm, walking away from us.

"Wait." Zickar sent me a surprised look before rushing to catch up to her.

I followed, taking his hand and squeezing it. I felt like our lives were about to shift sideways, and I wanted to be with him when it happened.

"What do you mean?" he asked Tenkaril softly. "Dakur . . . My brother. He's dead. Alwen saw this. She watched as they buried him."

"And I have seen what she did," Tenkaril said. She gave me a nod. "You gave me hope, daughter, that all will be as it should." Tenkaril shook her finger at Zickar. "But no running off to the Ember Clan even if they discover what I suspect. We need you here too much, as does your growing youngling."

Gasping, I placed my hand on my belly. I was pregnant?

"Mate," Zickar said, his arm tightening around me. "Tell me, Mother. What question will Wambak ask of the Ember Clan?"

"The male Alwen saw in the cage, the one *I* saw through her eyes?" Tenkaril grinned, though it held a hint of sadness. "It wasn't Dakur."

I hope you enjoyed Zickar & Alwen's story!
Next is Orc's Captive, and I bet you've already
figured out it's Dakur's story!
Get Orc's Captive now!
Turn the page for Chapter 1...

Would you like to read a bonus epilogue
for Orc's Maiden?
Sign up for my newsletter, and get
it free! It's been two months, and
Alwen's about to fly on a vox . . .

ORC'S CAPTIVE

Can a wounded orc hero protect his treasured mate from a cruel captor?

Nia: I spend my days healing those forced to battle in my stepbrother's arena and my nights hiding. I've resigned myself to the fact that with my burn scars, I'll never find love. Until my stepbrother commands me to heal his latest acquisition—an orc who was severely injured during capture. I've only heard of orcs, but I do my best to heal him and prepare him for the battles he'll soon face.

As I care for Dakur's wounds, we exchange glances that slowly grow heated. It's not long before I'm falling in love for this gruff, stoic warrior who's as trapped here as me.

Can we find a way free to finally be together?

Dakur: I barely remember being captured, and I've suffered since, forced to fight in a ring while humans bet on the outcome. The only good thing in my life is Nia, the human woman who sparked my clan's pendant. She's my fated mate, though I doubt I'll live long enough to be with her. But as we fall deeper in love, I know I must find a way.

I'm going to get us out of this trap, and then I'm claiming Nia as mine.

Orc's Captive is Book 4 in the Monster Mate Hunt Series. Expect a seductive orc hero with a creative. . . (cough), size difference, a fierce, scarred woman who will do anything to protect those she loves, plus a fantasy world you'll want to live in. HEA guaranteed. Each book is standalone, but the series is more fun if read in order.

Trigger: Nia lives in a dark world, as do the creatures she heals—those her stepbrother forces to fight in the arena. There is no animal death on the page, however. Her stepbrother is mean. He pushes and threatens her.

Monster Mate Hunt

Books in Order:

Orc's Mate

(a prequel novel –

FREE with newsletter sign-up)
Orc's Craving
Orc's Fate
Orc's Maiden
Orc's Captive
Orc's Taming

ABOUT THE AUTHOR

Ava Ross is a two-time *USA Today* Bestselling author who has written numerous titles, all of them featuring sweet and steamy romance. She fell for men with unusual features when she first watched Star Wars, where alien creatures have gone mainstream. She lives in New England with her husband (who is sadly not an alien, though he is still cute in his own way), her kids, and a few assorted pets.

Also by Ava Ross

Series by AVA

Mail-Order Brides of Crakair

Brides of Driegon

Fated Mates of the Ferlaern Warriors

Fated Mates of the Xilan Warriors

Holiday with a Cu'zod Warrior

Galaxy Games

Alien Warrior Abandoned

Beastly Alien Boss

Bride of the Fae

A Sci-Fi Holiday Tail

Monsterville, USA

Monster on Board

(co-written with Alana Khan)

Love at First Orc

Monster Mate Hunt

Sweet Monster Treats

Brides of the Zuldrux Warriors

Monsters, PI

Single Titles

A Monster Worth Fighting For

Craving Stardust

Dad Bod Dragon

Mated to the Dragon

Jasmine's Enchanted Genie

Swamp Thing (You Make My Heart Sing)

You can find her books on Amazon.

CHAPTER 1
NIA

They called me a monster, but I preferred to think of myself as a mouse. I was tiny, pretty much defenseless, and I could barely resist bolting when anyone came near. Could I be blamed for the latter? If I didn't move fast enough, I'd feel the impact of a fist or the gouge of a blade.

As I hurried down the hillside outside my village after collecting herbs, I rubbed the network of scars on my neck and the right side of my face. I'd long since healed—on the outside. I wasn't sure I'd ever feel healed where it counted most—on my soul. When I looked in the mirror . . . Was it any wonder the villagers called me a monster?

Honestly, the true monster was my stepbrother.

Slinking through the back door of the compound I'd called home since my mother and stepfather died, I paused in the shadows and listened, hearing nothing but the thump of my heart. My breaths were uneven, but that was the norm. Until I'd locked my bedroom door and collapsed on my tiny bed, my breathing would remain erratic.

Keeping my footsteps light, I slunk through the dark hallways with only the soft glow of a whisp lantern to light my way until I came to the door leading to the network of underground passages.

Creatures fought and died down there. So did people.

And this was where those I cared for saw past my exterior to the kind heart I kept hidden from everyone else.

I tiptoed down the wooden stairs, my footsteps echoing around me, only punctuated by a groan or sigh of pain from an injured being. It hurt to think of their wounds and the slashes on their hides.

But I did what I could to heal them.

After slipping past the room where the guards sat playing cards, I moved down the long, narrow hall with walled cages on each side. I stopped at the first and stepped inside, blankly taking in the stone walls, the dirt floor, and the bins containing food and water for the beast. Each was as trapped inside their cage as I was in the compound.

The beast's breaths rose and fell as he lay with his head on the ground and his eyes closed.

When I stepped forward with my basket of herbs and healing supplies hooked on my arm, his head snapped up, and his feral, black-glowing gaze met mine. He scrambled to his four hooves, grunting when his back right leg wouldn't support him.

His low growl rang out.

"It's me, precious one," I whispered, stepping toward him with my hand stretched out.

He sniffed it, and his body relaxed.

"I've come again to help," I said softly, lowering my basket to the floor.

He nudged my hand playfully before settling on the dirt floor once more, his wounded leg extended out beside him. This wasn't the first time I'd helped him, and it wouldn't be the last, or I hoped it wouldn't be the last time, because the alternative was a horrifying death in the arena.

One day, I'd make sure these poor souls were free— and myself, if I could make such a thing happen.

Other than escaping, there was no way out of this trap for either of us.

I made quick work of cleansing his wound, then covering it with a poultice I made from the herbs I'd collected. My only training came from my grandmother, and sometimes, it was all I could do to remember what she taught me before she died when I was ten.

Not long after that, my mother married my stepfather, and I "gained" an older stepbrother, Brunt.

When my mom and stepfather died in the fire, Brunt took over his dad's businesses and the arena. The compound had been here for a very long time. It was built when the village was initially settled, but I didn't know much more about its history than that.

After wrapping a bandage around the beast's leg, I went to his head and gently stroked his furry cheeks, staring into his soft dark eyes.

"I'm sorry I couldn't find any pain-relieving herbs," I said with an ache in my chest. "But I hope your laceration soon feels better. The poultice will help."

He nudged my belly with his snout and huffed out a breath.

My eyes stung. If only I could do more for him.

After making sure he had enough water and food, I moved on to the next cage. It took hours, but by the time the sun was setting, I'd finished helping all I could and returned to my room.

I couldn't do much else for them, but I hoped what I did gave them a brief moment of comfort.

Until night fell and they were forced into the ring once more.

Inside my room, I washed my hands in the basin.

While I didn't often dare, tonight, I stared at my image in the small mirror mounted on the wall above the wash cupboard, taking in my pale, almost white hair, my light blue eyes, and the network of scars puckering across the right side of my face and neck. The bands of distorted pink flesh stopped below the top of my blouse. I'd survived the fire when my mom and stepfather hadn't, and for that, I was grateful. Better to be scarred than dead.

After dressing in a clean skirt and blouse, I left my room and moved silently through the hall to the kitchen.

"There you are," Veegar said with a wry smile, looking back from where he stood at the stove preparing the meal for Brunt's men. I'd help him with this task and then serve what we made on big platters in the adjacent dining room. Veegar tilted his head to the plate sitting on the counter. "That's for you. Eat it before you do anything else."

My eyes watered once more. "You didn't have to do that. Bread and cheese, plus maybe an apple, would be enough."

"You deserve to eat as well as the others," he said softly, adding more meat and roasted vegetables to my plate. The spicy scent made my belly rumble, reminding me I hadn't eaten since dawn. "Take it to your room if that makes you feel better. I've got almost everything ready for the main meal. I'll collect your plate later."

"I'll bring it back." I hurried over to grab it and an eating implement.

His dark face beamed as he smiled down at me, revealing his fangs. There was a time when this male had taken his place among my stepbrother's warriors, but he'd aged and, thankfully, was assigned to the kitchen rather than tossed out onto the street. A wise move since Veegar was not just a strong warrior, but he was also an amazing cook.

Inside my room, I sat on my bed and ate, savoring the rich spices and subtle flavors Veegar gave each dish. He was wasted on Brunt and his crew. He should be running a restaurant in a big city. Although, the only city I knew of was many weeks of walking from here. Our village had been built near an oasis in the middle of an enormous desert, and other than a few migrating orcs who kept their distance as they passed outside the village limits, I'd seen no one but the descendants of families whose relatives settled here ages ago.

Finished, I'd set my empty plate on the low table beside my bed and was sliding off to take it back to the kitchen when someone banged on my door.

The knob rattled.

My heart leaped into my throat, making it a challenge to swallow. "Yes?" I squeaked.

"Get down to the beast area," my stepbrother barked. "Now."

"I've already cared for everyone."

"Not this one."

Ah. So he'd brought a new one in, had he?

One of these days, a beast would go feral and kill him. While I knew it was wrong of me, I looked forward to seeing him lying still on the dirt floor, maybe within one of the cages, while one of his "fighters" ripped him apart. He deserved it after what he did to them.

"I'll go," I said in a high-pitched voice. If I didn't quickly agree, he'd break down the door and make sure I understood the importance of following through on his commands.

"Now." With that, his footsteps moved away.

I gathered my things and, with the plate in my hand, scurried to my door, unlocking it to peek out. Spying no one in the hall, I hurried to the kitchen, though Veegar wasn't there. I could hear him in the dining room, serving the men and my stepbrother. Boisterous calls for more ale and food echoed in the adjacent room.

If I was lucky, I could take care of the wounded animal and get back to my room before they drank too much ale. My stepbrother wasn't good about protecting me from his men when he'd had too much to drink. Without alcohol, the only one he didn't protect me from was himself.

With my basket hanging over my arm, I sped down the steep stone stairs, the coldness sliding off the walls, sinking into my bones and rattling them. At the bottom, I paused and composed my face into a mask of indifference. It never paid to show that I felt affection for those I healed.

"Come to see the new one, have you?" The head guard, Kengart, asked, his gaze traveling down my frame, though without a sneer. One corner of his lips twisted up, making the knife scar spanning his face from his left temple to the skin below his right ear twist.

"Yes." I kept most of my attention on his feet. Eye contact was often seen as an invitation to touch. While Kengart left me alone, and my stepbrother's men had a healthy respect for his fist, they weren't above a grope here and there.

"I'll come with you," he said.

I shrugged. It hardly mattered. Like always, he'd get bored while I washed the beast's wound and leave before I'd finished dressing it. If I was lucky, he'd join the others in the guardroom and have a drink, forgetting all about me.

We passed the open room where three other guards played cards, bottles of ale on the floor beside their chairs. They drank while on duty, though never to distraction. My brother's fist wasn't the only thing they invited if they slacked off and got too drunk while they were supposed to be working—as Kengart's face had discovered over a year ago. I'd tended that wound as well, and my stepbrother's knife had cut to the bone. Kengart had been kind to me ever since, as kind as he could be while working under Brunt.

Once we'd passed the guardroom, my footsteps lightened, though it never paid to relax completely. Even in my room, I could only sleep when the door was locked, and my traps were in place.

Kengart moved lazily down the aisle between the cages, not even glancing through the tiny circular windows to see who might be inside. I paused at a few, watching to make sure those I'd helped earlier appeared comfortable and were resting.

"He's in here." Kengart waved to the last cage on the right, the only one without a small, barred window looking out into the hall. He opened the door and stepped inside the dark room with me following. "Looks like he's still unconscious." Trying to see in the dark, I only vaguely heard the concern in Kengart's voice. "Since he's still out of it, I'll leave you alone with him. But call out if you run into trouble."

Many of the beasts could be vicious at first, but this one, like all the others, would sense that I didn't mean harm. Some of the guards called me the beast whisperer because I could walk up to any creature be it tame or wild, and it would never bite. They must be able to tell I would never hurt them.

"Thank you," I said softly, keeping my eyes trained on the dirt floor.

Kengart only remained with me for a moment before stepping back out into the hall.

I waited until his footsteps retreated before shutting the door. None of them were locked. No need to do so when every creature in the cell block was chained.

Taking a whisp lantern from the hook near the door, I blew across it to make it flare. I turned, expecting to find another beast penned in this horrendous place, writhing in pain.

My breath stuttered from my lungs when I spied a wounded orc wearing only a scrap of leather over his groin. He lay on the low bunk mounted to the back wall, a thin blanket covering him to his mid-thighs. Like many in my stepbrother's menagerie, or "pets," as he laughingly called them, the orc was chained at his ankles and wrists. He had enough chain to stand beside the bed and move about, but not enough to reach more than halfway across the small room.

My heart on fire, I watched him, wondering if I dared approach. It was one thing to gently care for a wounded creature, another to go near an orc. Rumors about them crowded out every other thought in my mind. They killed others easily. They were a primitive, nearly feral species. And they captured women and abused them before tossing them aside.

Were the rumors true?

A sheen of sweat covered the green skin of his face and bare, heavily muscled torso, and he thrashed his head, murmuring words I didn't understand. His hair hung about his face and neck in limp, dark strands threaded through with smoky lavender.

I crept closer, taking in the deep laceration on his left shoulder, the big bruise on his temple. More bruises covered his chest, abdomen, and his strong thighs. My heart pinched at the sight. They'd beaten him, probably while capturing him, and from the pus leaking from his wounds, they'd left him untreated from the time they subdued him.

"I'm sorry," I whispered. "You shouldn't be here." Neither should I, but we were both captives in this horrible place.

I lowered my basket to the floor and reached toward him, only to pull my fingers back when he shifted on the bunk, groaning.

His eyes snapped open, and his dark purple gaze clouded with pain met mine.

He wore a metal pendant made up of a five-point

star, and as he shifted on the bunk to face me, it slid along the strip of leather encircling his neck.

As if it caught the light from the moon and stars shining down from the night sky so far above this gloomy compound, the pendant blazed.

The orc carefully lifted it, staring in awe as it flickered with light.

"Mate," he growled, his gaze locking on mine. His eyelids fluttered before closing. "Mate."

Get Orc's Captive NOW